"You and John have nothing in common."

Susannah looked at Morgan in exasperation. "Oh, you and your classifications. You sound like a psychologist. It's out of character."

Morgan laughed. Mischief lighted his brown eyes. "And who made you such a judge of my character? You don't know everything about me, by a long shot. How do you know I don't take pleasure in primitive urges like this, for instance ...?"

He pulled her close, bent his head, set his mouth on hers. His hands were warm against her shoulders through the thin silk shirt. She couldn't struggle. Morgan held her so close she was afraid he would hear the pounding of her heart.

Then suddenly she was aware that his heart was pounding, too.

Harlequin Salutes...

Essie Summers

Many of these titles are available at your local bookseller.

For a free catalogue listing all available Harlequin Romances,
send your name and address to:

HARLEQUIN READER SERVICE,
M.P.O. Box 707, Niagara Falls, N.Y. 14302
Canadian address: Stratford, Ontario, Canada N5A 6W2

Harlequin Salutes...

Spring in September

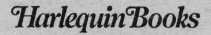

TORONTO•LONDON•NEW YORK•AMSTERDAM
SYDNEY•HAMBURG•PARIS•STOCKHOLM

Original hardcover edition published in 1978
by Mills & Boon Limited

ISBN 0-373-02148-8

Harlequin edition published March 1978

This *Harlequin Salutes* edition published March 1980

Printed in Canada

CHAPTER ONE

Susannah Carew stood in the Canterbury street not far from the great cathedral and listened to the magic of bells pealing out over the ancient city of pilgrimage. After an idyllic English summer this was the very first evening to hint that autumn was about to shorten the twilight, dim the clear vistas with silvery haze and turn the emerald leafiness of Kent to gold and russet.

September was a lovely month all over the world. Irresistibly her thoughts turned to the Southern Hemisphere, to another Canterbury, a province, peopled and nurtured by English settlers in the past century ... turned to memories of New Zealand Septembers, where daffodils would crowd the banks of the Avon in Christchurch and cherry-blossoms would soon deck the boughs. In the Millbrook Reserve crocuses would carpet the turf with mauve and white and gold chalices. Near the coast snowy white lambs would be gamboling, but south of Christchurch, nestled against the foothills, the lambs would just be arriving. It was too dangerous to lamb early there, with the Alpine snows so close. At Larchwood Vale, loveliest spot of all in Susannah's eyes, was all she held most dear with the exception, of course, of mother and father. But her mother's roots were there, and some day, when her parents' service to their country was at an end, they would return there to retire.

Perhaps it was because her parents lived such a cosmopolitan life that she was so attached to Larchwood. Her mother had been a fourth generation descendant of that pioneer family, but had followed Chris Carew all over the world in his Trade Commissioner posts. To compensate, they returned to Larchwood Vale every few years for extended leave.

The Canadian post he'd taken up so recently would be his last. It was departing from custom for Susannah not to have gone with him as his secretary, but she now had plans of her own, and in any case her parents had felt she must stay on to show Stephanie and Brent Morley around Britain, when these Larchwood neighbours had at last come to the country.

Susannah had revelled in it all, the beauty and wonder of the contours and history of this motherland she herself had loved so much this long while since. It had been mainly joy, therefore, except for those times that Stephanie spoke of the folk in that other Canterbury at the bottom of the world, unknowing she was touching an old scar, outwardly healed, but still tender.

Suddenly it was night, with stars pricking the sky. She must return to the hotel. She walked slowly. She came to a spot where she always stopped to pay tribute to one long-since dead, the remnant of the church where, on the twenty-sixth of February, 1564, Christopher Marlowe had been baptised. The poet who had written in his "Passionate Shepherd:"

> Come live with me and be my Love,
> And we will all the pleasures prove
> That hills and valleys, dale and field,
> And all the craggy mountains yield.

Long ago that had meant a lot to young Susannah Carew. Not now. Not any more. She'd never sigh for a New Zealand shepherd again. She'd come a long way since then, met a great many men. A traitorous thought crept in. None had ever stirred her pulses as had that southern shepherd one starry night in a September spring long ago. She gave herself an impatient shake. She wasn't a vulnerable twenty-two. She was twenty-seven with a world of experience behind her. She sauntered no longer. She walked briskly back to the Chaucer.

Stephanie and Brent were relieved to see her. Brent said, "I know you're familiar with this place, Shanna, but I'm not keen on you wandering dark back streets by yourself—they're so narrow. Besides, we've a proposition to put to you. We've asked sandwiches and tea to be sent up to our room."

Susannah thought it would be some travel project, some alteration of their plans for the short time they had left in Britain. Perhaps they wanted to take a final farewell of Suffolk, Stephanie's birthplace. But it wasn't. Stephanie came to the point right away. Had she hemmed and hawed, Susannah might have suspected the folks back home had put her up to it.

"Shanna, we know you're aiming for Canada, but your father said in his last letter he's very pleased with this secretary—might she be able to stay on with him? Because we'd like you to travel back to New Zealand with us. Mother wrote me today—I picked up the letter when you were out. Clothilde is planning another shipmates' reunion. According to mother Clothilde had said on the phone, 'Can't they persuade my grand-daughter to come back with you? I'm sure she's not as indispensable to her father as she thinks. I know her mother can't come to help organise it but if Shanna could, it would mean so much to me.' "

Susannah was surprised. "But the last one was just five years ago. They only have them every decade. Isn't that a bit much?"

But Brent said, "Clothilde may not be with us in another five years. Sorry to be so blunt, but we have to face that. She's the only one who can talk to the descendants of the other shipmates about their forebears, because of them all, only she has had it by word of mouth. And every celebration, someone turns up who couldn't make it before and wants to hear shipboard tales recounted by someone who learned them at Gerard Larchwood's knee. Clothilde had a letter from some descendant living in Alaska, of all places, who is to be here about that time on busness—oil, I think—and wants to meet her. That started it. She said to Steph's mother that she couldn't face it if you weren't with her to organise it, the way you did last time."

They lapsed into silence, pouring more tea, eating their sandwiches, as Susannah looked over their heads into the far corner of the room. Yes, last time she'd organised it quite creditably, with the help of Morgan, Stephanie's brother. It had been time-consuming, of course. Time that John had therefore spent in the company of her cousin from Tahiti, as someone had pointed out to her. But Morgan, with his innate kindness, had saved her face in that situation, had given her a way of releasing John without causing too much pain to that closely knit community.

Although the three estates were so large that the houses lay some distance from each other, the isolation of the early days had forged links of friendship that had lasted through generations. The Larchwoods, the Foresters, the Hervington-Blairs. The first ones had been three single men, who had formed this bond on board ship. Wilfrid Hervington-Blair was making his second trip to the new colony. He had returned to England to marry his betrothed, only to find that in his absence she had become attached to someone else. He was to thank his Maker all his life that she had. But at that time, his disappointment had made him determine to take up the most inaccessible land he could, beneath the mountains across the far, inhospitable Canterbury plains. His shipmates, Eldred Forester and Gerard Larchwood, had gone with him, granted land that was to be stocked within a certain time of their arrival.

Each of them had created pastoral beauty out of stony pastures, had tamed the wilderness, and each succeeding generation had added its own measure of loveliness to the valley, till autumn had brought gold and russet to an evergreen land, and prosperity where frugality had once been the order of the day. John had been a Forester, Stephanie and her brother, Hervington-Blairs. Oh, yes. Morgan Hervington-Blair had saved face for Shanna all those years ago.

Now she decided on candour. It would be a thought uppermost in everyone's mind when she returned, so why not bring it out into the open? "I'll come. But there's one thing I'll have to face. Everyone will think I've come back because Fran is gone. I'll hate that, and so, I imagine, will John."

Stephanie looked astounded. "I never thought of that. After all, *you* dumped John. It wasn't as if *he* jilted you for Fran. You dumped him because you'd fallen for Morgan. Then that didn't last, either—a pity from my point of view, as there's no one I'd rather have had for a sister-in-law. I see what you mean, though. Since you and Morgan parted, people might think you might make it up again with John. But not to worry. You can soon disabuse their minds of that. And in any case. . . ." She stopped dead and didn't continue.

Susannah looked at her curiously. Stephanie was normally such an uninhibited person. Susannah prompted her. "In any case what?"

Stephanie still seemed at a loss. Brent came to her aid, "Shanna, if my wife has second thoughts, I never probe. She's rash enough in speech, even the second time around." His wife threw a paperback at him and they all laughed.

Finally Stephanie said, "I earned that unenviable

reputation in my salad days. It's just shocking how things cling. And after all, the main thing is that Shanna's consented to come. Let all the gossips think what they will. Come to think of it, they might think you were still more interested in Morgan.''

Susannah laughed. "They might at that. They probably regard me as too fickle, though.'' She paused, then said, "Don't write and tell them immediately, though, Steph.''

Stephanie's face fell. "Shanna, you aren't having second thoughts? Oh, you couldn't? Please don't.''

Susannah didn't reply at once, and suddenly Stephanie said, "It's hard to realise that in a week we'll be setting off. Pity Morgan can't be there to meet us.''

Susannah bent to pick a crumb up off the carpet. "Morgan won't be there? Why not?''

"Because he's in the New Hebrides, working.''

Shanna couldn't have been more surprised if Stephanie had said her brother was at the South Pole. "Morgan . . . working in the Pacific? What on earth's he doing? And why haven't you told me?''

"I don't think you asked after him.''

"Didn't I?'' (Of course she hadn't . . . but this was astounding news.) "I never dreamed of him being anywhere else but at Larchwood Vale. Fancy grand-mère not saying.''

"Well, I daresay Clothilde's getting like all old people—a bit forgetful.''

Shanna agreed, though it was hard to think of her grandmother, with her inborn French shrewdness, being forgetful. "But what's Morgan doing?''

"Training some of the New Hebrideans in agriculture, animal husbandry and so on. And of course Dan Cairns has been at the Vale so many years now, he's just carried on.''

Shanna was aware of a peculiar expression on Brent's face. What could it mean? It had disapproval in it, puzzlement, uneasiness, she thought. Or was it just her imagination?

She switched to John Forester. "How is John coping? I expect it's not as difficult as if he and Françoise had had a family, but it's never easy for a man on his own. From time to time I've heard of him from grand-mère, but not much. It seems this housekeeper they had when Fran was ill, stayed on."

"Yes, she's a pet. Her husband isn't able to take full charge of the farm when John's absent, but he's a good overseer and keeps the garden beautiful. John's adjusted reasonably well. Not that you ever know exactly what John is thinking or feeling. He'll go in for politics eventually."

Politics! How different from the old days. The valley had seemed to be all John's world then, just as it had been the young Shanna's whenever she was left with her grandmother, those times when schooling was impossible where Chris Carew's missions had taken him. These five years would have changed John, just as they had changed Shanna. No doubt he'd needed something to take his mind off his loss. Farming routine left a man's mind too unoccupied. But if one was engaged in pitting one's wits against opponents, searching out new ways of solving old problems, sponsoring causes, seeking reforms, there would be fewer empty hours.

It was two years since Fran had died. Suddenly her image was before Susannah, in all its red gold and blue— the sun shining on that coppery head, the deep blue of the mountain skies reflected in her eyes.

Marty Griffiths had said to Shanna one day, "It's so lovely that you and Fran are such pals. Even if it was you who gave John up, it would have been natural had you resented him consoling himself so quickly, but it's just lovely to see you and Fran together. Cousins aren't always as close as this."

Shanna had laughed, glad to the depths of her being that no one had guessed the truth, that no one suspected that the love she and Morgan were supposed to have found for each other so suddenly was merely a face-saving pretence, so she said lightly, "Why on earth should I have wanted John to wear the willow for me? My conscience is eased this way."

Morgan had known John and Shanna were pledged to each other in everything but an official engagement, and it had been nothing but innate kindness on his part, sensing the trouble in Shanna's face as she watched John and Françoise together, that had made him offer her an easy way out of the coil. Susannah had grasped it eagerly.

They'd told John together that Shanna wanted to be free because she and Morgan had discovered they loved each other. John had acted admirably, showing no sign of relief, nor overdoing the spurned-suitor act, and not till the reunion was safely over had he let it be seen he was finding comfort in Fran's company.

Françoise's father, a wealthy businessman in Tahiti, had flown over for the reunion, and because of this Fran and John had decided to get married soon after it, so he might be there. Shanna stayed on quite a few weeks. Her parents were in Asia on a very delicate mission and had preferred to leave their daughter safely at Larchwood Vale as long as possible.

Then old Clothilde had complicated things. She had offered Morgan the managership of the estate. It was natural for her to think that one day, when she had passed on, her granddaughter's husband would run it. Susannah, knowing the temporary nature of their relationship, had expected Morgan to refuse. He hadn't. He'd put his thriving veterinary practice up for sale most promptly.

When they were alone she had asked why. He hadn't answered her for some time. When he turned back to her his lips had had a derisive twist to them. "Because it suits me very well to be manager here, Susannah Carew, why else?"

She'd gulped. "But to give up your veterinary work? You've loved it so much."

"There's one thing I love more—the land. Plenty of other vets have done just this. Gone through all that training to find the old hunger for your own acres dies hard."

His *own* acres. Something in Susannah had flinched from what that could mean. She said slowly, "That doesn't sound like you. It sounds . . . scheming."

He'd laughed shortly. "There are many things you don't know about me."

"So it seems. But . . . but what about Blair Peaks? It was a disappointment to your father all those years ago, I was told, when you didn't want to carry on after him, but he thought you might, in time, return to it. So why not, if you feel. . . ."

"You don't think I'd sink that low, do you? Brent looks on Blair Peaks as his own now. So he should, having managed it for years. Stephanie, too. Oh, I got part of my cut out of it to buy my practice, and I'll get the rest of my share in due time, though I hope that day's a long way off. When Brent and Stephanie moved into the second house on the place it was on the understanding that it was permanent. So what better than a manager-ship on Larchwood Vale, adjoining the acres my forebears farmed?"

Till then Susannah had thought their pretence at being engaged had occurred simply because of a chivalrous impulse on his part. Now she wasn't so sure. Was it possible Morgan had banked on this becoming reality? In that case he was due for a shock. It made it easier for her to break the engagement when the time came. She made it sooner than planned and flew off to join her parents in Bangkok.

She had expected him to take the practice off the market, but he hadn't. He had become manager of the Vale. But now, seemingly, he had suddenly thrown everything up. She ought to have been told. Her grandmother must indeed be getting vague. Or had she written and told mother? But would mother have overlooked passing that news on? Dan Cairns must have succeeded him as manager. Oh, what odds? It would be easier to go home now. To stay. But she had said nothing as yet about anything permanent. Her thoughts halted at that. Perhaps now was the moment to declare her intentions. In a relieved tone, she said, "Well, it's one less complication that Morgan's not there. I'd hate people to watch the three of us and wonder which one I'd pick. Now, maybe, I'll be free to live my life how and where I want to. And *where* is at Larchwood Vale. *How* is doing what my grandmother has done all these years . . . run the estate. It would make mother very happy. Before they left for Canada she said she'd try to get dad settled with someone so I could go home."

Again she had the impression that Stephanie was checking eager speech and having second thoughts.

It was still September, but spring, not autumn. Their long flight across the world was ended. They looked down from the jet on to the chequerboard of the Canterbury Plains in rich greenness, rimmed by a blue Pacific, and bounded to the west by the wide tangle of mountains that was the Southern Alps.

They glided in, there was a puff of smoke as the tyres touched the tarmac, and Susannah knew the incomparable gladness of homecoming. It was early morning and they spent just long enough in the city for Brent to pick up the new car he had ordered before their visit to Britain, then they were off on the Main South Road, till beyond the Rakaia River they would turn west and head towards the ranges.

Presently tarseal gave way to the rougher shingly roads, and the dust rose, but before them beckoned the shining silver heights dwarfing the foothills, so what did dust matter? The paddocks were full of fleecy lambs, gambolling with the sheer joy of life, just past the hazardous birth-time when late snows could blanket the plains and chill winds whistle through the gorges.

Today sunshine smiled upon daisied turf and sparkled on the water-races that saved the plains from the threat of drought in the scorching summers. In all the homesteads daffodils danced in the light zephyr and the sun shone through their translucent petals turning them to living gold.

Ribbons of grape-hyacinths bordered the flowerbeds and in the orchards already bridal white and bridesmaid pink were breaking on the leafless boughs. Ranunculis patched the gardens with red and gold, forsythia made golden fountains in the corners and white geese moved majestically in files towards ponds. Shanna's eyes swept the peaks, each contour known and loved . . . Mount Hutt, Mount Somers, D'Archiac, the Two Thumb Range, that looked so deceptively small from this distance. . . .

From Rakaia, though the plains seemed billiard-table flat at first, there was the faintest rise towards the Gorge, but now they turned southwest and could see the road rising steadily as they sped towards the cleft in the foothills that sheltered the three homesteads. Soon they could discern them, Larchwood Vale standing proudly in the centre, in whitewashed stone, with blue shutters, a gracious old Colonial house. Blair Hill homestead was to be distinguished to the right, farthest of all, and nearer at hand was Forester Gorge Estate, its home trees paler green than the surrounding native bush, marking the spot where, in its sheltered garden, John Forester's homestead was situated.

A long drive led up to it. They would pass the massive stone gateway soon. Shanna felt nothing as she raised her eyes to it. Once, so long ago it belonged to another existence, she had thought her future lay at Forester Gorge; it had seemed idyllic, so close to her adored grandmother. They turned the bend, there were the gates, and beside them, a tall dark man on a tall dark horse. John.

Brent slowed up, stopped. John swung off his mount, on Susannah's side, opened the back door for her, and said, "Welcome home, wanderer." He touched her cheek lightly with his lips. He brushed Stephanie's cheek, too, and greeted Brent. "I thought you'd be here about this time, so I went around the sheep on this side of the hill. Saw your dust from up there. Clothilde is all excited, of course. No, it hasn't been a bit too much for her. She shed ten years after I rode over with your letter, Stephanie, to say Shanna was coming home."

Stephanie had thought that was best—for grand-mère's sake, she'd said. Had it also been that she'd wanted to tell John his first love was coming home? Shanna flinched inwardly at the thought. She hoped they wouldn't suffer from the matchmakers.

She said crisply, "Well, we mustn't dally. Grand-mère will have the binoculars out in the Eyrie, and she'll be impatient. See you in a day or two, John."

"I'm driving over tonight—a gathering of the clans. Your mother and father are already there, Stephanie. Your mother's dying to hear first-hand, instead of just in letters, what you thought of Suffolk, if it's changed."

As always at the thought of Stephen and Marian Hervington-Blair, Shanna knew a rush of love. They were so sweet. Impossible to believe they were in their seventies. They had been childless so long, then when Marian had been nearly forty she had had Morgan, then Stephanie, so they appeared to be in a younger age-bracket.

The last bend, then the gateposts carved in larchwood sprays from stone on the estate. An immense wattle so symmetrical it looked like a golden ball stood at one side, an enormous beech only now uncurling its first brown-green leaf-buds to the spring, on the other.

Memory stirred in Susannah. Morgan had said once, in the short time of that sham engagement, "That's the colour of your eyes, Susannah—not quite brown, not quite green, but somewhere in between." She couldn't remember John ever comparing her eyes to anything. Now Fran's eyes had been sapphire, sea-blue, the colour of deep summer skies. And Fran's hair had been red-gold like fine spun copper wire, whereas Shanna had been a towhead. Just tow. No wonder Fran had outshone her in John's eyes.

Otherwise, feature by feature, they had been so alike. It was like seeing twin portraits, one hung carefully to avoid fading, the other exposed too long to bright sunlight. Or so Shanna had told herself.

But all that had finished five years ago. She wasn't so vulnerable now, she told herself. These last years had been crammed with experience, full of gaiety and social occasions, and she'd met many men. And, she told herself fiercely now, the only reason she'd felt so desolate, so forlorn, even though light-hearted on the surface, was because in all this world travel, which so many people envied her, she was parted from Larch-wood Vale, the spot she loved best on earth.

Her hungry eyes took in the scene before her, searching for signs of change she would have resented, and finding none. The post fences gleamed as whitely, the Larch Water ran as sweetly over its shallow rocky bed, tinkling down in a succession of leaps from the rock-garden, daffodils clustered under the silver birches by the old water-wheel ... there was still a tree-house in the weeping willow, still the sound of hens clucking contentedly, let out on free range after their morning laying activities.

Sheep and lambs dotted the lower hillsides ... there was a gleam of rich purple through the poplars where Clothilde's violet patch would still scent the air. The camelias were in full bloom and sun shining on the pussy-willow catkins turned them to pure silver. They rounded the bend of the drive and swung around to stop at the foot of the terrace steps. A slender figure was seen hurrying down to them with a glad disregard of the

chance of tripping and the hazard of what ought to have
been the feebleness of eighty years and more, but wasn't.

Susannah was out before the car quite stopped and
rushed towards her grandmother, arms outstretched to
catch that darling figure, should it hurtle down. They met
on the third step up. Clothilde folded this loved
granddaughter to her and held her as if she'd never let
her go again. But finally she held her off, said, "But oh,
what *chic*! That time on the Continent has taught you a
thing or two, *chérie*! Though you always possessed a
knowledge of how to wear your clothes, even those so
abominable jeans . . . and how to walk. Eh, but it does
my old heart good to see you. I would like to meet the
designer of your suit. He must have had someone like you
in mind when he created it. It is the colour of new beech
leaves, greeny-brown, or is it brownish-green, with here
and there a touch of dark honey-colour for your hair?"

Shanna flicked her grandmother's cheek. "Oh, grand-
mère, you'd make anyone feel a million dollars! This
elegance is in your honour, of course. I know better than
to arrive in comfy but disreputable cords. But I'll be into
them very shortly, I warn you." She saw the gleam of
tears in the faded blue eyes, knew her own were misty,
said crisply, "I'm simply starving after that drive. Is the
kettle on?"

Clothilde Larchwood said, "The Hervington-Blairs
are here. They're presiding over the teapot. The tea
should be ready now. Come into the drawing-room, all of
you."

Clothilde would have scorned to call it a lounge,
modern style. Shanna linked her arm in her grandmother's. The wide French windows were open on the terrace;
the drapes in lilac and purple were blowing a little. It was
rather dim inside after the brightness without. So that at
first Shanna saw only the two Hervington-Blairs she'd
expected, Stephen and Marian. But not the third. Not
Morgan.

So it would still be a triangle: she, John, Morgan. He

came forward, pecked at the cool cheek she turned hastily. Susannah said, "I thought you were an apparition, that you were in the New Hebrides. How come you're here?"

"Where else would I be? I had just a couple of months there. Surely you wouldn't think I'd be away in lambing."

Susannah turned to Stephanie. "I thought you meant Morgan had left the Vale altogether."

Stephanie looked puzzled. "Did you? How could I have given you that impression? Though I thought he was still over there."

Susannah looked at Brent. He had been there when Stephanie said that. He chuckled, "I usually clarify my wife's woolly statements, Shanna. Seemingly I didn't this time. But if ever Morgan left the Vale I'm sure it wouldn't be for life on a Pacific island—no sheep! If there's one thing that's certain, it's that he's a sheepman."

"I suppose so," said Susannah lightly, "though with such a varied experience as a vet, I've not exactly thought of him as so dyed-in-the-wool—forgive the pun. Now John would be a different proposition altogether. Nothing but sheep."

"Don't you believe it," said Morgan. "Sheep certainly, but also politics . . . plus a few other diversions." His tone was dry.

She dropped her handbag on a stool. "Now I want some tea. I don't know what it is about the Canterbury Plains, but I get a craving for tea the moment I look down on them."

Marian Hervington-Blair began pouring. Stephen beamed at their daughter, newly returned to them. "I've never seen you look so well, Stephanie. You've got a bloom . . . England must have agreed with you."

"It did," said Stephanie, a lilt in her voice and a sparkling look at Brent. "I'm a late starter like you, mother. There's a baby on the way."

They were all delighted, and Shanna was glad the conversation then became centered on Stephanie and Brent. She sat beside her grandmother, glancing now and then at the contours of that well-loved face. Time hadn't marked it much in the last five years, she was happy to see.

Morgan handed her a plate of pikelets. "Come on, eat up," he said brusquely, when she shook her head. "It's not much fun for the ones who prepared the fatted calf if the Prodigal Son says he's gone off veal. Besides, you can't be dieting. You're too thin already."

She grinned. "After near-starvation and husks, I can't imagine the Prodigal Son turning roast veal down, wisecracking guy. I've had two of those already. I'd like some of your mother's shortbread—I recognised her designs, the wheat-ears and the Tudor rose. Takes me back to the first time I ever noticed them, when I was twelve." She reached out for a piece.

"When you were twelve," said Morgan, "and plagued the life out of me. It seems a long time ago. You were so adventurous I seemed to spend my days doing nothing but fishing you and Louis out of sheep-dips or cattle-pens, or getting you down from tall trees. You could shin up in great style, but always got stuck coming down. When I wasn't doing that, I was shielding the worst of your misdemeanours from your grand-père. I used to wish you'd attach yourself to someone else."

Shanna decided on candour. "I had a crush on you," she explained. "I thought it was heavenly when you helped out here that month. You were my hero. I was completely fascinated with the way you managed sick and enraged animals. I used to lie awake at night and dream of handing you your heart's desire on a golden platter."

Morgan looked astounded. "My heart's desire? What, for instance?"

Well, he'd asked. Susannah looked mischievous. "Like doing something to make Marty Reddington realise you were the better man, and ditching Philip Griffiths for you.''

Morgan's mouth fell open. "Marty Reddington? My heart's desire? Ye gods! That was only a flash in the pan. I took her out a few times, for sure, but she made it so plain very soon where her interests lay, I'd no time to get deeply involved. I'd no idea I'd ever been a hero to you.'' He laughed. "Then when you came back for the last reunion when you were twenty-two, you had to fall for John. Pity you switched your allegiance as things turned out.''

Shanna accepted another cup from Morgan's mother. That gave her a little time to consider her answer. "Oh, I don't know. You didn't expect pre-teenage hero-worship to last, did you, Morgan? To survive a decade? And John was more my contemporary. Oddly enough, at twelve he'd not made much impact. Perhaps because I had Louis. But suddenly, the next time. . . .''

"Suddenly your common sense deserted you and you went overboard for *him*.''

They measured glances. Their voices became low, intense. "Morgan, once that would have made me flaming mad, but not these days. What could cause you to make such a contemptuous remark? John's steady, reliable. What do you mean, common sense deserting me? Anybody would think I fell for a rascal.''

"Well, if you don't know that John wasn't the chap for you by now, I couldn't convince you.''

Shanna said, "Pass me one of those ginger kisses, would you? Oh, thanks. You're surely not basing that judgment on him because he happened to fall for Fran . . . these things happen. We weren't . . . quite . . . engaged.''

The brown eyes in his tanned face were watchful, trying to read her reactions, she thought.

He said, "I voiced my doubts about his being a suitable husband for you long before that. That night we read Gerard's letters to his Victorine, remember?''

She had her own reasons for not wanting to remember that night. She said levelly, "But that was merely asking me if we—John and I—had kindred tastes, not speaking of him in contempt."

"I wasn't contemptuous of him *then*. I merely thought you were throwing yourself away on him." Morgan paused, eyes still on her face. "Oh, perhaps then it was just sour grapes. It's hard to be impartial when you see the other fellow making his wicket good."

Susannah looked swiftly down. But . . . but . . . that was before he had noticed John looking warmly at Fran and had made his face-saving suggestion to her? A bitter realisation swept over her. When you were the only grandchild and heir to a big estate, it was almost impossible to be sure if you were being sought out for yourself, or for your prospects.

She raised her eyes and was quite proud of the steadiness of her voice. "Is it possible, Morgan, that it wasn't just a chivalrous impulse that made you act as you did, that day? That it wasn't just to save my face? That your motives weren't as disinterested as you made out?"

"You've got it right at last," he drawled. "More perceptive than you used to be. I merely saw the opportunity I was looking for and took it. But you remained so completely and foolishly unaware—might as well admit it now. But you wouldn't play ball. You used me for the time, then skipped it."

Shanna took a hasty sip of tea. She'd almost choked—but not on a crumb, on resentment.

"Well, I admire your honesty. Pity you weren't as honest five years ago. And you thought it might have worked out?"

"I did."

Her voice matched his for coolness. "How? Why?"

This time he seemed to hesitate. Then, "Let's just say it would have helped give me . . . on that golden platter what I most desired."

Susannah drew in a deep breath. What a pity they

weren't alone. She'd have scorched his ears...He wanted Larchwood Vale as much as that! Of course Stephanie and Brent had been settled in on the Blair Hill Estate for years. It had been what seemed an ideal solution to Stephen Hervington-Blair when his daughter had married a farmer. Morgan could have had the farm, years before that, but had chosen to train as a vet, and obviously regretted it. Larchwood Vale was the next best thing. And she had actually been naïve enough to think he'd thrown it up and gone off to some new, challenging work in the New Hebrides.

She came out of her thoughts to hear Morgan say, "So now you're home again. And the water that's flowed under the bridge these last few years means that John is free again. Don't make a fool of yourself over him again, Shanna. I won't step into the breach this time if you do. Haven't the years taught you anything? Given you some discrimination? Haven't you stopped seeing that Adonis with rose-coloured spectacles yet, Shanna?"

She said, with a derisive note in her own voice, "That's not very apt, Morgan. If a chap is an Adonis, one doesn't need rose-coloured spectacles."

"Well then, bring reason to bear upon the situation. You'd never make a go of marriage with John Forester. Have some sense."

"Sense? Would it have been sensible to enter into marriage with you?"

"Yes, we could've made a fine thing of it. We have kindred interests, the sort of attachment that lasts into old age. Like father's and mother's, for instance. Not just a romantic flame, something that might burn out, but a kind of hearthglow. Steady, warm, comforting."

Shanna felt chilled to the core, but she said levelly. "You picked the wrong pair for your comparison, Morgan. Your father and mother had both. When I was twelve, I was at Blair Hills one day when your father came home a day early after a week at a farmers' conference. I was up in your room getting a book. I was

dipping into it on the dormer-seat. I heard the car and
looked out. Your mother came flying out like a schoolgirl
and positively cast herself into you father's arms. I liked
it. I thought they had it all, the flame and the hearthglow.
Not that I thought anything so highfalutin' then. I just
felt in my bones that this was indeed true love."

"Then what a pity when you were so far-seeing at
twelve, that you were so blind at twenty-two to fall for
someone as shoddy as John Forester!"

The curl of her lip was hidden from the others,
fortunately. "But at least I was discriminating enough to
put a quick finish to our sham engagement, Morgan."

She put her cup down, turned to the rest of the room.
"Grand-mère, I just can't wait to see everything, every
nook and cranny of the house . . . say we leave the Blair
Hill folk to their own intimate family reunion, and make
a tour by ourselves?"

She'd have liked Morgan to look set back. But as she
left the room she heard him say easily, "Tell me about
that visit of yours to the Ancient House in Ipswich, Steph.
You're not much of a letter-writer, you know, but you
can talk a blue streak. I hope some day to visit it myself
and see where Charles the Second-to-be was hidden
before he escaped to the Continent."

Shanna wished passionately that Morgan Hervington-
Blair had never come back from the New Hebrides.

CHAPTER TWO

Susannah hoped grand-mère wouldn't notice anything. It took her the entire tour of the top storey before she could stop that mist of anger rising in front of her vision. She told herself it was because he had sneered so at John, dear honest, uncomplicated John, who perhaps lacked some of the interesting facets of Morgan's personality, but mightn't be the worse for that. John who should have known a lifetime of serene happiness with Françoise and who had had only three short years.

Who did Morgan Hervington-Blair think he was? The complete answer to any woman's ideal of a husband? Oh, these bachelors! They became so self-sufficient, so smug!

Clothilde said mildly, "I asked you, *chérie*, if you didn't think it was extraordinary that after all these years that same pattern chintz came back?"

Shanna said hurriedly, "Oh, sorry, darling. Perhaps I'm suffering from jet-lag after skipping the date-line. The same pattern as what?"

The shrewd old eyes twinkled. "Jet-lag, is it? Well, it covers up, I suppose. Never easy to meet an ex-fiancé . . . and you seemed to be having quite a deep conversation. I strained my ears, but the others were drowning you out. It's the same pattern Victorine Larchwood used for her curtains when they moved from the sod-hut into this. I remembered it as a child, of course, when my mother used to bring me here from Akaroa, for the holidays. I made sure by taking in her old work-basket. It was lined with a piece. I was so excited. Of course this is even better material. It has a bit of terylene in it. Perhaps it will last even more generations. Or will some future mistress of Larchwood Vale despise an old-fashioned design like this?''

A strange feeling assailed Shanna. Some future mistress who might not care for old, well-loved and tended things. Who might even deem the old house had had its day and pull it down. An immense pity struck her for her grandmother, who had lost the two sons who should have succeded at Larchwood Vale—the Second World War had seen to that. Who was faced now with knowing that some day this lovely old home might fall into strange hands, even cease to be.

Clothilde said, gazing out through the mauve and rose chintz, across the smiling acres that sloped down to the plains, "History had a way of repeating itself in the Larchwood family . . . till now. First Gerard Larchwood seeking his bride in French Akaroa rather than in English Christchurch and bringing Victorine Rossignol here in 1862, and then their grandson wedding me from there. We'd played together as children. I believe our parents and grandparents thought then how ideal it would be if we married. And it was.''

Shanna said, "Grand-mère, one looks at one's forebears' unions and never questions their happiness or success. Children seem to think such marriages were meant to be. And I suppose that looking back over many years, one could forget early misgivings. Was it always ideal for you? Did you want to marry Grand-père Humphrey and no one else? I mean, with the French, arranged márriages were quite the thing? Did your parents and grandparents bring pressure to bear? Was it a case of them thinking it ideal, and you going their way?''

Clothilde burst into such a peal of laughter it was irresistible, and Shanna had to join in. "Oh, child! I was only terrified that their matchmaking would put Humphrey off. I was in love with him at eighteen, and he went away to the First World War. I was sure he'd fall for some French girl and never come back, even if he survived that hell of trench warfare. I thought that with his being so fluent in French, he was just bound to be popular. I think all those years of separation made our years together doubly precious. We'd known what it was to be without each other. I read once that 'No woman is worth very much until she has been through a good deal of sadness, a great deal of wanting that which she cannot get.' I'm sure I was the better for my long apprenticeship with pain and longing.

"Your mother knew that too. I suppose she told you she wanted so much to marry a farmer, to strike roots deep down? She just wouldn't let herself love your father at first. My girl was deeply unhappy for a long time and I couldn't find out why at first. When I did, I had to tell her that women have always followed their men and found it worth while, that I knew that from my own experience. I'd hoped as a child I'd never be beyond sight and sound of the sea. I had to come inland, far inland, but for Humphrey's sake I actually came to love the mountains more. It's wonderful, I daresay, if a woman can have the setting she loves *and* the man, but don't ever let that influence you, *chérie*. Don't be afraid of this return of yours. If in these years away you have formed an attachment for someone on the other side of the world, then that is where you must be. In time you'll know your own heart . . . and where you should be.''

Shanna looked southwest where the gables of John's house could be glimpsed through the trees. She said,

"You mean I just might find my happiness within sight of Larchwood Vale? That I ought not to mind if I was a second choice?"

"That I did not say," said Clothilde firmly. "I said you would know your own heart in time. I've never been fond of overloading the young with advice. One can only bring them up to recognise true values and goodness and to hope that they will act upon such judgment. You would do well to forget that you once were engaged to Morgan to save face, my little one, when you became aware that John was attracted to Françoise. Here at the Vale we've always marked time by decades. Humphrey's grandfather used to say we all got a fresh start then, but I thought ten years too long for you this time, *mignonne*. In five years not only John has changed. So have you. So has Morgan. Couldn't you see them both with new eyes, Susannah?"

Shanna didn't answer that. She seized on something else. "Grand-mère . . . you knew that was a put-up job? Our engagement? Did Morgan tell you? It was supposed to be our own secret."

"He had no need to tell me. I knew from the start. I was in the shrubbery when Morgan offered you that sop to your pride. And now I'll tell you I prayed you'd never break that engagement."

"But we knew it had to be broken. It was just a stopgap."

"I thought you might find it so sweet, so satisfying, you'd never let him go."

"It was never sweet. Never satisfying. It was bitter-sweet, grand-mère."

"Isn't all love bitter-sweet? I remember. I've never forgotten what it's like to be young. Isn't unalloyed sweetness too cloying? I know. But the young demand such perfection, such instant happiness, when instead it has to be achieved hour by hour, day by day, year by year."

Shanna felt moved and didn't want to show it. She

said instead, "Grand-mère . . . you knew, didn't you, that it wasn't just a knightly gesture to save my face? That Morgan really wanted to marry me for reasons of his own. That he seized that opportunity?"

"I did, and thought none the less of him for that, and neither should you."

"Grand-mère, I'm not with you in that. To me it was unpardonable to appear chivalrous when it was opportunist."

Grand-mère shrugged. "We must differ, then. You are too analytical, *chérie*. But don't hold it against the Morgan of today. A man's mistakes of yesterday should never be held against him. Me, I have never believed that forgiveness was worth a sou without forgetfulness. Perhaps he blundered. Take it from here, blotting out what happened five years ago. Be happy in just being home, little one."

At that moment they heard Morgan's voice. From downstairs he called, "Mother and father and the rest are off to the Peaks now. Come and say goodbye!" So the three of them would be left alone. Not a gathering of the clans as John had suggested. But he was driving over. She hoped so. . . .

He didn't come. He rang. They had had dinner by then, prepared earlier by Clothilde and served, unexpectedly and deftly, by Morgan. He'd looked at Clothilde with sheer affection. "She mustn't get overtired on your first day home. Besides, it's the thing now for the men to pitch in and help too. Help at this distance from town is non-existent now. We have a woman coming in two days a week, but she's an amazing worker and accomplishes a terrific amount of the basic chores in that time."

He and Susannah had washed the dishes and settled down in front of a fire of bush-logs. Outwardly all was amity. Morgan answered the phone. "For you, Susannah—John." He held out the phone to her.

The greenish eyes met the brown ones squarely. There was a hint of challenge in each. She said coolly, "Leave it off the hook till I get to the other phone, Morgan. Much more private."

He didn't lower his voice so Clothilde couldn't hear. "Good heavens, I didn't dream you'd need privacy now! Okay, I'll bash it back as soon as you speak."

Shanna was certain grand-mère turned an escaping laugh into a cough. Oh, but she was a naughty old lady getting fun out of a situation that wasn't funny at all! She said "John?" and the next moment, after an ear-splitting crash he said, "What on earth's going on? Someone knocking something over?"

She laughed. "No, just Morgan's heavy hand replacing the other receiver. I'd rather take the call in the hall."

John laughed, "That takes me back a number of years, Shanna, when it was always that way."

Something else was the same for Shanna too . . . the caressing quality of his voice. She was rather surprised she remembered it so vividly. She said crisply, "But the reason was different, John. I know I wrote when you lost Fran, to express my sympathy. Now that I'm here in person I'd like to underline it, and I felt you wouldn't want the others within earshot. I was glad to see you looking so well today. I dreaded meeting you, because to lose someone like Fran must have cut right into your life and I felt it could have changed you so much."

John said, "Well, life goes on, and one recovers. I'd learned that long ago. When you gave me up."

Shanna was silent. She'd not expected that. She'd lived so long with the knowledge that he'd been attracted to Fran before she gave him up, that she hadn't expected him to refer to it as if Fran had been a consolation prize.

She managed to recover and say lightly, "Well, of course Fran had dawned on your horizon so very opportunely—it didn't take long, did it?"

He said quickly, eagerly, "Shanna, did it hurt that I consoled myself so quickly? I always wondered, especially when you finally broke it off with Morgan. I mean the engagement didn't last long, did it? I wondered if I'd waited you might have found out it was just an infatuation; a girl often does fall for an older man, then it fades. I wondered whether you might have regretted that engagement.''

Regretted! Oh, no, only the manner of it, the fact that they had known from the first impulsive beginning that it would end before too long. But even now she wouldn't have forgone a moment of those bitter-sweet weeks. She tore her mind away.

John said, "I'm sorry I'll not be able to come over tonight after all. I have to go down to Ashburton to a very hastily convened political meeting. Anyway, I guess you're tired. How about one of our old-time rides tomorrow morning? Morgan's grey should suit you nicely. You will? Good. Meet me at the Crag, Shanna, at six. Grand-mère doesn't breakfast till eight these days. Morgan gives it to her in bed. It's her one concession to age.''

Shanna didn't know what her reasons were for consenting to that revival of a custom, meeting John in the early light at the Crag. She didn't want to admit it was sheer willfulness. To show Morgan? To show him what? She wouldn't answer that, even to herself.

She kept any hint of bravado out of her tone as she went back into the room. "Morgan, may I have your grey tomorrow morning for an early ride, or will you be needing her? John said she'd be all right for me, but if you. . . .''

"No, you can have her. I don't go around the sheep early these days. Dan does the first round. But I'll be up. I'll saddle her for you. Meeting John?''

"Yes, at the Crag, like we used to do. Then I'll know I'm really home.''

"Yes, nothing like old customs for making you feel you've not been away long. But don't jump any fences till you've had a bit of practice. Well, I'm off.''

She said quickly, "Oh, don't feel you have to leave us

alone on our first night, Morgan. I noticed you've a
sitting-room as well as a bedroom but do stay here.''

Grand-mère spoke for him, "Oh, he's off to Ngaio
Bend. Philip Griffiths is away in Australia and Morgan
has to help Marty fill in the stud records.''

Shanna thought, but did not say, "How nice for
Marty.''

When he'd gone she said, "How is Marty these days?''

"Oh, more beautiful than ever. Her hair is still the
same bright copper, her eyes that glorious blue like
Fran's eyes. Her children are adorable. Dorothy and
Roberta are like her, in looks and personality. Like
quicksilver. Richard is like his father, and his grandfather after whom he was named, and almost as tall. Peter
is ginger and freckled and an imp. They're growing up.
The five years since you've seen them has made a great
difference. Marty is freer now, of course.''

Very free, thought Shanna, with Philip in Australia
and Morgan filling in. At the end of the evening she said,
"Do we leave something out for Morgan, grand-mère?''

"No, he'll have something with Marty. And he'll be
late.''

He certainly was, though Susannah wasn't yet asleep.
She was lying in the dark, her mind teeming. Oh, how
stupid it was to have found the evening something of an
anti-climax, because Morgan was at Ngaio Bend and
John in Ashburton. But as soon as she got her teeth into
the hundred-and-one details for the reunion, the
catering, the invitations, the entertainment, she'd feel
different.

When she heard Morgan's car purr into the barn, the
moon, freeing itself from a bar of cloud, shone through
her undrawn curtains. A full moon, with one attendant
star. Just such a moon as had appeared over the tips of
the larches in the garden that September night five years
ago, the first of their engagement.

They had walked through the larch copse that
symbolised the name of the property, because to give

colour to their pretence they'd wanted to give the impression that solitude and a world of two was desirable to them.

They had come to a full stop as that long-ago moon had, as now, freed itself of cloud and looked down on them. Beyond and above them the everlasting mountains had reared, the light silvering the snow-shawl on their shoulders. The mint-like fragrance of the pennyroyal they had crushed beneath their feet came up to them ... Shanna could smell it now ... but then, because the beauty and intimacy of the scene had shaken her, she'd said derisively, "Back at the homestead they're probably thinking what a perfect night for lovers!"

Morgan had turned to her, said, "So it is ... what a pity to waste it, Susannah. Let's get all we can out of this and to the devil with John Forester!" He'd caught her to him, kissed her quite passionately. It was the first time she'd ever known his lips on hers. He'd often pecked her cheek in greeting.

She'd been taken unaware, hadn't put up a guard against response. Because he'd no idea that she'd been going to give John up in any case, before he butted in with his misplaced chivalry. She had given herself wholly into his embrace. For her it seemed as if the very stars swung with the magic of it. In that moment she knew how right she had been to halt on the brink of accepting John. Then as Morgan lifted his head he said "Wow! I'm certainly getting my reward for saving the lady's face, aren't I? John must be mad to prefer Fran!" And with that ill-starred remark, the magic had faded and Shanna knew the taste of ashes.

Now she was furious with herself again. Had the last five years taught her nothing? Did it take only the sight of a September moon to set her pulses racing, her heart longing? It was nothing but spring fever and the joy of homecoming. She ought to have stayed in that other Canterbury where the year was drawing slowly to a close, where leaves were beginning to yellow, instead of coming her where the sap was rising in the heart of the trees and turning the leaves to living green. Spring was a foolish time, a dangerous time.

She heard a horse whinny. That would be Lady Grey hearing Morgan go by. She heard his voice speak to the mare, just a murmur, then his footsteps on the brick cobbles of the courtyard. Now he whistled as he came, softly. That was the custom here when the men came home late at night, to reassure them it was no stranger of evil intent approaching. But did he have to whistle *that*? But he'd probably forgotten the association. Perhaps it was subconscious, a matter of habit.

He'd found the poem in one of his mother's scrapbooks not long after their engagement and because he was a musician of no mean ability he'd set it to music. She hadn't read anything into that, because Morgan was always hunting for verses to write a score for. He used to make up nonsense rhymes for her and Louis all those years ago, but said he was no hand at serious poetry so had to use other people's lyrics. A Tasmanian poet of years before, one Norma Davies, had written it. The poem had been called *September Moon* and had begun:

Something too wonderful to tread the world;
Something too beautiful for human hands to
  hold . . .

He'd played it to them in the drawing-room, with grand-mère and his mother and father nodding sentimentally. Now Shanna fitted the words to his whistling, as unaware she was awake and listening, Morgan Hervington-Blair came home.

He came to the two last lines . . .

While in the mystic smile you earthward turn
Gold memories of dead Septembers burn.

Was he remembering one September night, one
September moon? Or were such memories well and truly
dead? Oh, Susannah Carew, don't be such a fool. He's
coming back from Marty whom he loved long ago, no
matter what he said today. Marty who was nearer his
own age, not like little Shanna whom he'd rescued from
predicaments so often as a child that it had become a
habit . . . and that, coupled with his own land-hunger,
had brought about that situation. Go to sleep, Shanna,
you're quite, quite crazy. You thought it would be easier
to return if he wasn't here, and return you had to, for
grand-mère's sake, but idiot that you are, you're glad,
glad, glad he's here.

When her alarm showed her it was quarter to six she
rose, donned green slacks and a thick cream silk shirt,
knotted a green and gold scarf under the collar, tied the
thick honey-coloured streaky hair back into an absurd
two inches of ponytail because it wasn't really long
enough and, shoes in hand, crept quietly downstairs.

She opened the kitchen door to find Morgan at the
table, a pot of tea ready and sliced bread and butter. He
gestured towards it. She glanced at her watch, said, "No,
thanks. I'd better get going."

"Oh, don't be daft. Let *him* do the running this time. It
won't hurt him to wait. Don't let him get the idea you'll
come when ever he whistles. He's too used to that sort of
thing. It's that treacly voice of his."

Shanna said cooly, "If you're often like this, Morgan
Hervington-Blair, it's a wonder you've not gone through
life getting your face slapped. But I'll have some. It was
more that I couldn't be bothered sitting here listening to
you sharpening your wits on me."

"Not wise to ride on an empty stomach. And you
might be persuaded to stay out longer than you
anticipate."

"Not I. I'll be back at seven-thirty to make Grand-
mère's breakfast. Yours too."

"Don't put yourself out on my account. I've rustled it up for both of us for long enough."

"Don't be ridiculous, Morgan. Now I'm here I take over the housekeeping. That's the whole idea. Did you think I was going to play the lady?"

"I thought you might have continued on to the Gorge Homestead to look over the lie of the land there."

Susannah poured herself some tea, sipped it, then bit into a crusty piece of bread appreciatively. "I see grand-mère still makes her own butter. This has a lovely salty tang. The lie of the land, Morgan? Exactly what did you mean?"

"Well, don't you want to know if the housekeeper has dug herself in so well she may take some dislodging? That would be natural enough."

"Not to me. I'm not as scheming as you were—are—I even hesitated about coming back in case people thought I wanted to console John. Matchmakers are a menace. But you've already made up your mind that I've come here with that in view. As if anyone could take Françoise's place with John!"

"Who would want to?"

Shanna stared. "What an extraordinary remark! People get married again all the time, and it's right. Life can be long and lonely. And second love, I've heard, can be so sweet."

"Well, I guess if a chap makes a success of his first marriage a girl wouldn't be afraid to marry him, but few girls would want to risk being as unhappy as Fran was."

Shanna left the rest of her tea, and stood up. "Morgan! You go too far. I don't believe you. And why say such a thing?"

The brown eyes met hers squarely. "Because you broke your heart once over that suave devil. I wouldn't like it to happen again."

She turned at the door, tossing over her shoulder, "Know something, smart guy? I don't happen to believe in broken hearts. They only get bruised, and bruising's not fatal," and she was gone from him in a wave of anger, out into the blue and gold spring morning.

To the devil with Morgan Hervington-Blair! From now on he was going to mean less than nothing to her. She would *not* fall under his spell again. There was one thing: if he continued to behave like this, goading and baiting her about John, she would be completely disillusioned about him. That was a shocking thing to say about John's wife—that she had been unhappy. Suddenly it mattered horribly to Susannah to know that Fran *had* been happy, in spite of what Morgan had been saying.

Her cousin had had such a brief married life, three short years, and at the end of that time, had slipped out of life, with her baby daughter surviving her by just one hour. It was quite unbearable to think she might have been unhappy. Her thoughts halted, her doubts stilled.

Morgan was just doing this because he didn't want her to marry John and take from him a fine chance of some day becoming the owner of Larchwood Vale. He was prepared to do anything to attain that goal, even to be cruel, something she'd never have suspected Morgan of being.

It was therefore a shock to find this cruel man had saddled up his mare for her. Lady Grey was a little older, but still a magnificent animal with a dappling shaded from silver to slate. Shanna fondled her, then put a foot in the stirrup and was up. The breeze that swept from the Pacific Ocean, leagues away, cooled both her temples and her temper. The face of the countryside was glorious this spring morning. Shanna's spirits rose. Tensions and moods departed.

The sun from the east silhouetted John against the background of green shining native bush across the Gorge. The Crag rose behind him, like a miniature Rock of Gibraltar in shape, scene of their morning trysts five years ago, when she'd imagined she loved him. She'd wanted to fall in love with him because his land adjoined

Larchwood Vale, because if she married him, it would give her a stable background next to her loved grandmother.

For a few brief weeks it had been an idyll ... till Morgan had come more frequently to Larchwood Vale to assist with the preparations for the reunion. He'd taken on an assistant for his clinic, so he could spare more time to assist his mother and father and Clothilde. John had said he was too busy, and they knew he wasn't as interested as his people had been ten years earlier.

She and Morgan had worked together day after day, night after night, producing the history booklet, and somehow it had involved them all in an emotional tangle. John had found time to entertain Françoise while they were busy. As for Shanna, after so much time spent with Morgan, an articulate man, a well-read man, with a fantastic memory for Colonial history, she'd found the younger man's company insipid, uninspiring. She began to have doubts. Was this the man to spend the rest of her life with? Did he ever talk anything but farming, wool prices, subsidies, production, fertilisers? There was non of the quick give-and-take of Morgan's conversation. John could hold forth for ages, given a subject, but how much light and shade was there, how much variety?

She'd looked on the beautiful Gorge Homestead with new eyes. Till then she'd taken it for granted these were John's books, but on examination she'd found they were all his father's and grandfather's. There seemed no new one added, except for farming manuals. How different from Morgan's room at his parents' home, crammed with every possible type of book: novels, biographies, books on mountaineering, on social problems, poetry, theology, classics, moderns, books that jostled his own veterinary volumes almost off their shelves.

She'd begun to wonder what, if she married John, they would talk about in the long winter evenings, possibly isolated by snow, with power-cuts that would deprive them of radio, television, telephone.

Then came the night when, with a blinding flash, she'd known she loved Morgan Hervington-Blair. They had been searching for more records of the disastrous snowstorm of 1867, the worst storm in known history, when thousands of sheep perished and communications were cut for weeks, when stores ran out and they almost starved.

Clothilde had said that the first wife here, Victorine, had given a very graphic account of it in letters to her mother at Akaroa. Morgan said, "Then they'll be preserved over there, not here? Who would have them?"

Clothilde said, "They *are* here. Her mother said she must have them back, that in time to come, they would make history. The editor of the *Akaroa Mail* thought they ought to be published, but Lady Barker of Broomielaw beat Victorine to it and the accounts were naturally so similar, it was never done. They're upstairs in the boxroom. I'll find them."

She'd rummaged around in a really hideous old dressing-table whose only redeeming feature must have been the number and size of its drawers, and which bore the scars inflicted when it had been transported over the plains in a day and submerged in various river-crossings. There were several bundles of letters tied up with white tape. One had a slip of paper and was marked *The Great Snowstorm.*

Clothilde went downstairs again leaving them sitting on an equally hideous plush sofa in bottle-green with square insets of a floral design. They'd found items of great interest pertaining to the three homesteads in the letters. It was like finding a treasure-trove. They were just about to take that one package downstairs and were replacing the other bundles, when one slid out, different from the rest in that it had a white ribbon, embossed with a forget-me-not design, tied around it.

"Aha," said Morgan, "I suspect high romance in this package, don't you?"

Shanna opened the top one. "Oh, Morgan, these must

be the love-letters Gerard wrote to his Victorine when
she was in distant Akaroa and he was wooing her from
here. No wonder there aren't many—no post, of course.
These would be taken by someone in a saddle-bag, to
Christchurch, and the same way over the Peninsula Hills.
Oh, Morgan, I'd love to read them, but. . . ."

"But what?"

"Wouldn't it seem like picking the lock of the past?
Perhaps they're very private?"

"Susannah . . . it's so long ago, it couldn't hurt
anyone. Besides, if you could resist reading them, I'm
sure I couldn't. But I tell you what. Let's go down and ask
Clothilde. I'm sure those letters have been read before."

They ran down. Clothilde put her book aside. "Yes,
they have. By me, for instance." She chuckled. "Humphrey and I had had a royal fight. My fault, of course—
oh, the quick temper I had when young! He tried to
placate me, but I ran away upstairs, with him chasing
after me, and locked myself in that dormer. Humphrey
was really furious and clumped off downstairs and
slammed the door so hard the whole house reverberated.
I heard him whistle Jess and ride off. He went to your
place, Morgan, thinking I needed time to cool off. So I
decided I'd come down and make myself some tea. And
I'd read a novel, not do my churning.

"Oh, the scare I got when I couldn't get out!
Something had gone wrong with the lock. I thought he'd
never come home. Coming back, his horse cast a shoe. I
was sure he had been thrown, of course, and that he was
dead, and it was all my fault. I was glad to light a candle
and rummage for something to read to keep my mind off
the horrifying possibilities. I found those letters. By the
time I read the last one I knew, oh, so well, that I loved
Humphrey as Gerard had loved his Victorine. Poor
Humphrey! He knew I'd be out of my mind with anxiety,
but never dreamed I was a prisoner. You can still see the
marks on the door where he prised it open. By all means

read them, children, but not down here. Electric light is so prosaic. Go back up to the dormer with two candles."

Laughing, they did just that. There were only six in all, because in the last one, Gerard had thanked Victorine for being brave enough to face leaving comparative civilisation such as she knew at Rossignol Bay to dwell among the harshness of the mountains. Long before they came to that happy ending, they had become enchanted with Gerard's beautiful handwriting, his instinctive choice of vivid words, all revealing a mind well-cultured before he'd left the shores of England to venture everything in a new colony. He always included poetry in his letters. Susannah knew a swift envy of Victorine Rossignol, her great-great-great-grandmother. Oh, to have been wooed in those days! Days when men were articulate and not afraid of sounding romantic.

Morgan was reading them aloud. She was suddenly aware of his long-ago Welsh ancestry that gave a lilt to his voice. He said, "Oh, listen, Susannah. He says, 'There are so many things that enchant me about you, Victorine. You actually said in your last letter that you couldn't imagine what I saw in you. Well, when you look in your mirror, my love, you see hair the colour of *manuka* honey and eyes that are neither brown nor green, so perhaps I should call them hazel, and a small straight nose . . . perhaps if you smile at your reflection you might see a dimple in your left cheek (what ever happened to the other?) but that's about all you'll see.

"But I see the way you move your hands, I hear your voice with its French intonation and occasionally its quaint way of fumbling for an English idiom, and the curve of your chin, and your black ironwork earrings swinging. Most of all I love the way you walk. I wish I could write poetry. I've tried but am never satisfied. Fortunately someone, years ago, said it for me. This is how I feel, Victorine, about you:

She walks in beauty, like the night

Of cloudless climes and starry skies,
And all that's best of dark and bright
Meets in her aspect and her eyes,
Thus mellow'd to that tender light
Which heaven to gaudy day denies.

When are you coming to Larchwood Vale, Victorine,
so that we can be together all the time? Not only the
beauty of daytime to share, but also the magic of night.

All my love,
Your Gerard."

Susannah had felt a tremor run over her, a delight not
known before, and her eyes, looking up from that
ending, had locked with Morgan's.

He had known she was on the brink of becoming
engaged to John. But for that, she was sure he would have
kissed her. With a shock she realised she most
desperately wanted him to do so. She felt a warm colour
suffusing her cheeks and hoped it wouldn't be noticed in
the dim candlelight. To bridge the moment she said, "I
wonder who did write that."

"Byron wrote it, Susannah."

She looked up again. "I've just realized something,
Morgan. I've never known you at a loss for the source of
a poem. Grand-mère always just appeals to you when
she's doing a crossword. What's your secret? A
fantastically good memory?"

"I believe I have a good one, but it's more that I love
poetry and always want to know why a poet wrote
certain lines. So why and who and when are all mixed up
together."

It was at that moment that she became aware that her
affection for John Forester was no more than a tepid
bond; that it had been mostly wishful thinking . . . con-

ning herself into caring for someone who would keep her close to Larchwood and her grandmother.

They had stowed the letters away and had begun to descend the stairs. On the top landing Morgan had paused and swung her around to face him. "Tell me, Susannah, does John like poetry?"

She'd blinked. "I . . . I don't think so. He . . . isn't a great reader. At least, he reads on the subjects that interest him. But not widely."

"So you *have* realised that?"

"Yes. Why?"

"Just that I've been thinking about that ever since you went all starry-eyed about him. I wondered if you'd brought any sense to bear upon the attraction. Marriage is for life, or so we hope. Sometimes it can't be. But some of the breakdowns might never happen if a little reason is brought to bear upon the subject of compatibility. Analysis can be a good thing . . . putting aside charm, and sex, and a certain aura that clings to a dear and familiar setting, and finding out what else there is. The compatibility of the mind."

She'd been honest then. "I *have* thought about it, Morgan. That's all I'm prepared to say at this moment."

"It's enough to go on with. But don't, Susannah, get carried away by the old shipmates atmosphere of next month and think it would be romantic to unite the later branches of two of the first families."

"I'll bear that in mind," she'd said in a whisper, and they went on downstairs.

She had lain awake all that night, turning over this new discovery. How lucky she'd made it in time to prevent her saying yes to John. Much better a gradual cooling-off than a broken engagement which might rupture the bond between the two families. For a few days she had lived in a happy daze. She thought Morgan was just biding his time, that while he thought she was almost promised to John, he couldn't speak. But Morgan had remained distant and even the closeness of their task had brough no sense of intimacy.

She'd asked John to look after her distant cousin Françoise, who'd come over from Tahiti, and when she'd seen how John had looked at Fran, she'd known he wouldn't be broken-hearted when she gave him up. She'd watched them very closely one day, from a vantage point in the shrubbery, where she'd been picking rhododendrons, unaware that Morgan was in his turn watching her. And he had swept her into a pretence she had hoped might become real and true. How naïve she had been! Shanna shook her head as if to free it of these old hurtful memories and at that moment saw John cantering towards her.

CHAPTER THREE

There was nothing but pleasure in his greeting and all restraint vanished. He held out a hand, his dark eyes looking into hers. "Lets turn back the clock, Shanna, and ride as if we hadn't a care or sorrow in the world."

Her spirit, freed from dark recollections, responded. She wheeled around to level up with him, and said, the one dimple in evidence, "Right . . . what mark shall we take for goal?"

"Those cabbage trees by Gerard's Crossing. Away!"

He was a magnificent rider, with much show-jumping to his credit, but he didn't ride to his full extent this morning, knowing she'd not ridden for so long. But it was open country with few hazards, and how exhilarating it was. John drew rein before he reached the *ti*-trees with their cabbage-like tufted heads, and allowed her to catch up to him. His eyes were admiring. It warmed her heart after Morgan's hostility.

"Let's turn up here. We've bulldozed a track right up Black Beech Gulley and cut a splendid vantage point on the other side. We can get a great sweep with the binoculars there when mustering. You can spot the stragglers easily and send the dogs in after them.''

The horses picked their way carefully up the rough track, the jingle of the harness blending with *tuis* calling, bellbirds chiming, the mating call of a blackbird, the splash of waters in the ravine far below. They came out on to the new Lookout. Each side they got the useful view of smalled hills, and dead centre lay the whole shimmering plain.

John shaded his eyes against the brilliance in the east. "So different from the old days. Imagine the time it took our ancestors in the first generation to get to Christchurch! Now I can be at the airport there in under two hours and in Wellington for Wool Board or Wheat Board meetings in another hour. Once it took the first Forester three weeks to reach Christchurch because the Rakaia and Selwyn rivers were in flood. Even without floods or snow it often took Eldred three days. Yet if I go to Europe or Canada for trade discussions any time, I'll be there in less time than he took to reach Cathedral Square!''

"Might you be doing just that before long, John? Going to Canada or Europe?''

"Yes.'' He hesitated, then said, "I should certainly make it next year. I could have this year but fortunately Stephanie's letter saying you were coming home reached here two days before the deadline for acceptance came up.''

Shanna was startled. "You don't mean you turned it down because of me, John? Oh, you shouldn't. . . .''

"I do mean just that. Why shouldn't I mean it? I only applied because it would give me the chance of seeing you. It was to be Brussels, London, Canada, so even when I heard, after my application went in, that your father was off to Canada, it didn't matter. Even if you went with him, I'd see you somewhere.''

Susannah knew it was a compliment, but she was dismayed for all that. She'd just wanted this to be a homecoming, not an instant inward turmoil. John mustn't think it was going to be just as it was before Fran or Morgan complicated their lives.

She said crisply, "Couldn't you still take it? I mean, my decision to come home is so recent, it mightn't be too late. I believe you're getting very interested in politics, so wouldn't this advance you in that ambition? What a pity to turn it down."

The dark, unreadable eyes met hers. Once she had found that intriguing. Now she wasn't sure. "I don't count it a pity. Time enough for a trip like that later. I found it easy to pass up when I knew you were coming. Frankly, if a chap's given a chance to retrieve an old mistake, he'd be a fool to leave the field free for Morgan, who charmed you away from me once before."

Shanna felt breathless, but not shy. She met his glance levelly. "John, there's nothing between Morgan and me. We're just destined, as before, for grand-mère's sake, to work closely together. She doesn't feel she'll see another reunion if we wait the customary decade, so we must humour her. I want it to be a happy one for her. I don't want it to be as the last one was, a time of snarled relationships. And in any case, I can't . . . quite . . . get used to the idea that Françoise is gone. Oh, forgive me, it's much worse for you, but all my last memories of Larchwood Vale are bound up with Fran. We were so much more than cousins; we were friends. I loved her dearly."

John drew nearer so that his leg was warm against hers. She kept her eyes fixed on that distant scene. He said, "Fran's been gone two years. A chap has to take up life again, and never forget, my dear, that you gave me up. Fran comforted me, but you were always first with me."

Shanna bit her lip. "Oh, John, you'll have to know this. I'd made up my mind to give you up a couple of weeks or so before I actually did. By then, you see, I was pretty sure, and it was a great comfort to me that you were attracted to Fran anyway. But your saying this makes me very uneasy.''

He said sharply. ''Uneasy? Why should it?''

She turned and looked into the handsome face so close to hers, her eyes searching. ''John, I couldn't bear it if I thought Françoise ever looked upon herself as second best. Did she? Did she feel she'd caught you on the rebound? Because that would make any woman unhappy. I'd rather think that you'd said to her at some time that you were lucky I'd given you up, that you were glad we'd never actually become engaged. I myself told Françoise that it had never been a grand passion for either of us. I thought I'd convinced her. So tell me, please, John, was she unhappy because of me?''

His jaw tightened, ''Shanna, if anyone has hinted to you that Fran was unhappy, it wasn't because of you. Want to know what it was? Just homesickness. For Tahiti, for its warmth, its gaiety, its sunshine and colour. Perhaps I ought to have sold out and taken her farming in the sub-tropical north instead of continuing in this alpine region. But I thought, in time, as other brides have done here, she'd come to love it. That's all it was. Don't let anyone put any doubts about me in your mind.

''Oh, come on, Shanna, give it time. I shouldn't have spoken to you so seriously, so soon. But to be on the verge of going to seek you out, then to find you were almost on your way, got me off balance. And although Stephanie said it was because even shocks of joy can affect old people that she wanted me to tell your grandmother, I felt perhaps it was also because she wanted to tell *me* . . . that she may have heard from her people that I was in for this mission, and thought it a pity if we fetched up still on opposite sides of the world. She may have thought this reunion might bring us together again, just as the other parted us.''

Shanna had to accept that. Nevertheless she doubted if Stephanie would have had that in mind. She could recall how five years ago, Stephanie had wept when she and

Morgan had parted, had said how she'd have loved to have her for a sister-in-law.

They made their way down, parted at the Crag, John returning to his house, empty except for a housekeeper and her odd-job husband, she to Morgan, from whom she must continue to hide her real feelings. But one ache in her heart was eased. Françoise hadn't been unhappy in her marriage, only homesick, which was natural, and would have passed, if only she'd been given time. Instead she and her little Justine lay in one grave among the tombstones of the Larchwood Chapel, under these mountains, instead of where the blue Pacific lapped the shores of her childhood home.

She came into the house singing, to find Morgan with the table set and a tray ready for Clothilde. She braced herself for a dry remark that her gallop had done her good, but he merely turned from ladling porridge into a blue stripped bowl and said, "Good, you've timed it nicely. You can help me make this up. I'm sure the first thing Clothilde will want to set eyes on this morning will be her granddaughter. Otherwise she'll think she only dreamed it. I'll follow with the tray."

Grand-mère was sitting up in bed, a fluffy amethyst cloud of shawl about her shoulders, her blue eyes bright with anticipation, her cheeks flushed delicately pink, her white hair brushed and shining, and caught up with a tortoiseshell comb.

"Isn't she a vain old girl?" teased Morgan. "She always has nighties and bedjackets to match her pastel-tinted bedroom. You remind me of Tudor royalty, Clothilde, receiving courtiers in your bedroom."

He piled up pillows behind her while Susannah adjusted the tray. Grand-mère giggled. "Elise Rossignol at Akaroa would be ashamed of me ... so solid a breakfast! She still gets her croissants and cherry jam. Margot, Pierre's wife, indulges her whims. But when I came here I found the mountain air made me ravenous, so I shared Humphrey's breakfasts and it saved time. But these days I skip the bacon and eggs.''

Sharing breakfast with Morgan in the big blue and white kitchen seemed so domesticated.

Shanna said, "How is Tante Elise these days?"

"Oh, blooming. It gave her a new lease on life when Pierre and Margot built motels on the property and kept quarters for themselves in Rossignol House so that Elise would never have to leave it. There is a small Elise now, did you know?"

"Yes, they wrote mother."

"She's the delight of Elise's heart. They're all coming for the reunion, of course, because they're so intermarried with the Vale descendants, they wouldn't miss it for anything. Time's going to crowd in on us now, Susannah. Of course this time we're not burdened with writing up over a hundred years of family life on the plains."

Burdened? She'd never thought of that felicitous task as a burden. Hard work, yes, and a great responsibility because any errors that got into print were permanent, but it had been a delight, a gladness . . . a revelation. For her, anyway.

She pushed that to the back of her mind, and began to discuss details. Invitations had to be sent out early because this wasn't the expected ten-year event; Morgan's mother had most of the catering arrangements well in hand; his father had ordered a large marquee in case of rain to accomodate the children, though the rest of the guests could be entertained in the old ballroom.

"And Marty, bless her, has offered to provide entertainment for the children, wet or fine; they need to be organised a little. We went through some of the arrangements together last night after I'd finished my work on the stud book."

Jealousy, new to Shanna, flooded through her. When she had become aware that John had obviously fallen in love with Fran's copper-gold hair and sapphire eyes, she hadn't known a pang, only relief, but Marty, with the same alluring colouring, had once been loved by Morgan, no matter how lightly he might dismiss that first love now. Shanna envied her fiercly. Those two girls had had the sort of colouring that, compared with her own, was like juxtaposing harvest-moon light, and one pale candle! In Susannah's life men didn't prefer blondes . . . they preferred redheads!

Morgan said, "Why are you looking like that, Susannah Carew? As if you had an unpleasant taste in your mouth?"

He was too astute by far. There was an edge to her tone. "Who do you think you are? Sir Omniscience instead of merely Morgan Hervington-Blair? Able to read people's thoughts!"

He said impatiently, "Cut out this Hervington-Blair nonsense. Dropped it to Blair ages ago—too much of a mouthful. I only use it on documents these days. It ought to have gone out long ago, but in more class-conscious days it meant something."

"Where did it come from? I always wonder about hyphenated names."

"Back in the eighteenth century. A Blair from Scotland, not a rich suitor, paid court to the only daughter of the Hervingtons of Hervington Place and attached her name to his own so it wouldn't die out when they inherited the estate."

Susannah frowned. Then her brow cleared and she said, "Well, at least they left his name in at the last. Sometimes they made it the first. It was a nerve, wasn't it, for families to expect a man to drop his name entirely, even making it a condition sometimes . . . or the marriage wasn't on?"

He said mildly, "You sound all up tight about it. Why? How are you to know this was conducted in a hostile manner, with a pistol to the head? Consent held otherwise."

"Well, you practically said so. Naturally I inferred that it was a condition."

"Naturally nothing You're very aggressive this morning. I never heard anything of the kind In fact, the opposite. Murray Blair was so sorry for a man who had lost three sons, who had no male heir, and whose name was about to be lost, so he offered it. He was probably very fond of his Julia's father You never know, Susannah, when you eventually marry and give Clothilde a grandson-in-law, he might grow as fond of her as I am. He might offer to put Larchwood in front of his name, despised hyphen and all!"

Shanna finished her toast, and pushed her plate away "Names die out, places don't There'll always be a Larchwood Vale. I'd never ask that of any man. I'd wear my husband's name alone and be proud of it."

Morgan said, "That could be selfish. You aren't thinking of what it would mean to your grandmother. I think it's lovely in family trees to see names repeated over and over In fact in the short time of our engagement I—"

He was interrupted fiercely "Of our sham engagement!"

He took it equably "Of our *sham* engagement. I thought if you were sensible enough to see that marriage between us would work, and it would have pleased everyone at that, I thought we might keep a name from long ago and call our first daughter Victorine Rose "

Shanna caught her lower lip between her teeth to stop its quiver for a betraying second, then let it go. Morgan had thought that? Yet she'd once read that men rarely, if ever, thought of themselves as potential fathers, yet girls dreamed of motherhood from earliest years, and picked names for their future children from kindergarten days on. And that hadn't even been a genuine engagement

She managed to say, with a curl of her lip, "You really did have it all worked out, didn't you? A blueprint for marriage . . . anyone would think *you* were the one with the French ancestors. For goodness' sake, Morgan, when you go courting again, be a bit red-blooded about it. No wonder Marty—'' She stopped dead, aware that temper had betrayed her.

He finished it for her. "No wonder Marty preferred Philip. Well, I wouldn't disagree with that. I think she got the better man, though even they got their wires crossed for a bit. You've certainly changed since you were an engaging twelve year old, Shanna. I used to think it would be a lucky fellow who got you when you grew up, that you had the promise of a winsome woman. Who'd have thought you'd become such a shrew? Four years of living in the sophisticated centres of the world hasn't improved you at all. I used to think it could happen that when you and young Louis Rossignol grew up, you might marry. But of course he didn't come five years ago.''

Shanna's eyes widened. She ought never to have said that about Marty. Pride, however, made her say scornfully, "Louis! He's my cousin, and I don't believe in cousins marrying.''

"Heavens, Shanna, what sort of cousin is he? At least a forty-second. His branch of the family left Akaroa for Tahiti in the eighteen-forties. He was a grand youngster fifteen years ago. You've heard, I suppose, of his mountaineering exploits since? Mainly in South America.''

He had hardly ever called her Shanna He'd said, in those bitter-sweet days, that he considered it a crime to shorten a name as beautiful as Susannah. The only times he'd ever used the diminutive were when he'd been cross with her as a child. When he'd swatted both Louis and her for taking out the old punt on the house-dam, and the day, disobeying orders, she'd got too close to the hoofs of Demon Dan.

She said, still perversely, to mark her lack of interest in Louis, "I think I've heard that, vaguely, but didn't know much about him.''

His tawny brows contracted. "No, I suppose not. Haven't had much interest in the family the last few years, have you?"

Now she was really mad at him. "You must be joking! I've never failed to write to grand-mère once a week in all the years."

His tone was dry. "It's easy to write. That entails no sacrifice such as—" He stopped.

Her eyes went really green. They challenged his "Go on, Morgan. You've a pretty nifty knack of tongue-lashing yourself. A male shrew, in fact. Don't spare me No sacrifice such as what?"

He said slowly and deliberately, "Such as leaving the fleshpots, the receptions and diplomatic highlights, the travel in the beauty spots of the world . . . to come home to a gallant old lady who has never once moaned about loneliness, and would have been even more solitary but for someone no relation to her at all."

"You mean yourself, of course, Saint Morgan. I think a halo suits you."

He shrugged. "See what I mean? Definitely shrewish. You're quite a fighter. That's known as carrying the attack into the enemy's own camp, and I simply refuse to take you up on it."

She felt as if he'd stabbed her physically. Enemy? Morgan? Never . . . even when he was criticising her like this he was still the man she loved, had loved for five years. In fairness to him, and to herself, she ought to tell him she hadn't been free to come—till now.

The first two years, of course, she hadn't dared return, with Morgan on Larchwood Vale. She hoped he might have married someone else, then she'd have come home to stay. To stay in the place she loved best in the world. What were all the other beauty-spots compared to this? . . . The Bay of Naples, the canals of Venice, the fountains of Rome, the lake-washed beauty of Zurich, the enchantment of the Grand-Place in Brussels, at night, the austere charm of Moscow, what were any of them compared with the mellow dearness of Larchwood Vale, the forest streams singing as they descended to the plains, the fragrance of cabbage-tree blossoms scenting the dawn air, moonlight on her own mountains turning a winter night to a witchery of silver?

Then when she'd convinced herself she had rooted her love for Morgan out of her heart, she booked a flight back to New Zealand, but before she could announce her return, the threat of sudden and serious illness had hung over her mother's life. Marguerite, incredibly brave in face of so much pain and dread, had ruled that her mother was not to know. "If she knows she'll give up. There will be nothing left for her to live for. I'll manage to write as if things were just as normal, as exciting, as gay as ever."

She had managed just that, all through that time of exhausting treatment, surgery, convalescence, endless relapses. Then had come that miracle drug and complete restoration to health. For the last six months there had been no recurrence. But when Shanna had rung her in Canada to say she was going home and why, she had asked her daughter to say nothing yet. "Mother would worry. We'll come for the reunion and will tell her then. Otherwise she would worry, but when she sees me blooming with health, she won't."

But she'd tell Morgan now, to justify her own long time of no return. She said, "Morgan, you'd better know I had personal reasons for staying there. One has other loyalties—"

He held up his hand. "I guessed that. Some man—only that could have kept you there. But Shanna, it's still true that he who excuses himself accuses himself, and there was no reason why, in these days of swift travel, you couldn't have come home for, say, three months at a time. If you dare not leave a man for that length of time then he's not worth having. Not a very good picker, are you, Shanna? Well, I've work to do."

"Well, of all the nerve! You've been sitting there

upbraiding me and censuring for dear life, and now you're blaming me for wasting your time."

"I wasn't actually. In fact I don't regard it as wasted at all. I've been wanting to say that for a very long time—for years, in fact."

"How nice for you to get all that spleen out of your system! You'll work better for it. Hope you don't want any help outside today, though I'll assist you other days, in spite of this. But I want to spend the time with grand-mère and tidy up the place a bit. I guess this woman does her best in the time she can give, but it's not the same as one of the family doing it."

He looked over his shoulder as he went out the door. "But don't offend her, will you? After all, we'll be glad of her services again after you've gone."

It took Susannah all of half an hour to cool down and be able to present a serene appearance to grand-mère. Well, she wouldn't accuse herself again by making excuses to Morgan Herving—to Morgan Blair! He could damned well think what he liked about her! He seemed to *want* to judge her and find her wanting!

Grand-mère had dozed off, but stirred as Shanna came into the room. Shanna kissed her, asked if she'd like to stay in bed awhile.

"But no, *chérie*, I do not want to waste a single moment more of this God-given spring day. I feel as that man in the Bible felt when his son came home again. We ought to do something to celebrate. But what?"

"No, love. We won't tire you out with the dancing and the feasting. We'll leave that till the reunion when mother and father will be here too. But what's this about the Prodigal's return? You won't think of me like that, will you, grand-mère?" Had her darling grandmother nursed resentment as Morgan had? Not for the first time Shanna wished her mother had told grand-mère when the worst was over.

Grand-mère chuckled. "You ninny. I wasn't thinking

about the son's side, just the father's joy in his return. Child, I may have wished you might come, and to stay, but I knew so well why you couldn't.''

Shanna turned with the tray in her hands. ''You knew? Why, I thought you didn't have a glimmer of suspicion. You haven't said anything to . . . .''

Clothilde's voice was tender. ''Of course I haven't. I knew you didn't care to come back for fear of revealing yourself. But it won't matter now. He loves you dearly, never doubt that. But it was such a tangled skein. Let time take care of it, child. We shall get the reunion over. By then time enough will have elapsed. You will grow into each other's ways again. Why else did you think I decided to have a shorter time between the reunions? This time, I think, you have come home to stay, my darling *petite-fille.*''

Grand-mère didn't know. She didn't know mother's life had been threatened. She thought I stayed away because I couldn't bear to see John and Françoise together! Now she thinks I have a second chance to take my happiness there. Oh, if only she knew!

When grand-mère came down, she decreed they mustn't spend too much time inside on such a day. ''You must walk around the garden with me, *chérie*, exulting as I do in the miracle of spring returning to waken those shrivelled brown bulbs to rainbow-coloured life . . . you know how hard with frost the ground here gets . . . it is a miracle to see the earth cracking and then find one day a tiny spear-tip of green that some day will be a daffodil; to see the hard shiny buds on the weeping willows bursting forth as a little warmth gets into the sun, and this year we had that most magical of all things happen . . . do you remember, Susannah, what I've always loved most of all?''

Shanna considered it, then, ''Oh, grand-mère, a light fall of snow after the chionodoxa blooms . . . the glory-of-the-snow. I thought of you last spring—I mean, of course, the English spring this year. It was early April. I

took the train to Osterley to show a friend Osterley
House. We came out of the station on to the Great West
Road and in a plot on the pavement was a carpet of
glory-of-the-snow, like a blue and white pool, with
daffodils dancing above them.''

Clothilde nodded. "Someone told me long ago they
wouldn't grow up here. Then why are they called that? I
demanded. So with a lot of faith, and a little bit of good
horse-manure, I planted them, and year after year they
bloom for me.''

Morgan's voice was heard behind them, "And that
double-may above them was a happy idea, don't you
think? See. I take credit for that, seeing it was my idea.''

Shanna said, "I thought that was a bush of spiraca.''

"'That's its proper name. But so many people call
astilbe spiraea for some reason. It's less confusing, to say
nothing of sounding more poetical. For the same reason I
liked to call scabious lady's pincushion. Scabiosa sounds
like a skin disease.''

The sun shone through the tiny white rosettes on the
twigs of the may and behind it a flowering currant
glowed rosily. A tulip magnolia was opening its first rosy
chalice to the sun and violas and pansies purpled the
corners. "The late snowfall blackened the cinerarias
under the birches,'' mourned Clothilde, "but they are so
gallant, they'll come again.''

Iceland poppies danced in the slight breeze, black-
centered anemones were purple and scarlet by the front
steps, and from the plantation came the ceaseless
soughing of the pines.

Clothilde said softly, "That is what compensated me
for what I missed most at first, up here, the murmur of
tides lapping the shore. When I felt as if I couldn't bear a
moment longer not to see a blue harbour below Mount
Bossu, or feel a salt-tanged breeze against my cheeks, I
used to wander in the pine-grove and tell myself that the
first Larchwood wife hadn't even that sound to comfort
her ... Victorine planted every pine on that hillside,

while Gerard was trying to turn tussock into pasture. She had nothing but the evergreen bush in the gulleys till she brought a bit of Akaroa into the foothills above the plains.''

"Not only a bit of Akaroa," said Susannah softly, "but also a bit of Normandy. Those poplars were from Akaroa, therefore they are Normandy poplars, and those are Bourbon roses and French walnuts . . . when I visited Normandy two years ago, I picked a Bourbon rose and cried for Larchwood's roses.''

"And if legend is right," said Morgan, "and I think in this case it is true, those weeping willows by our brook are descendants of the ones near Napoleon's tomb on Saint Helena. You knew, didn't you, Susannah, that the willows around the Avon in Christchurch were taken from Akaroa which in turn claims its willows were taken there as willow wands from someone of French descent paying a pilgrimage there?''

She was Susannah again, which didn't mean she was forgiven, but just that Morgan wouldn't distress Clothilde by any hint that he and her granddaughter were at loggerheads.

They visited all the long-loved haunts, the fernery Victorine had created out of a hollow in the hillside, now a grotto-like gem where cascading waters made ceaseless music; the caves Shanna had loved as a child, the Watchtower Rock where Victorine had kept many long vigils, watching for her husband's safe return, knowing that when she saw the dust from his horse's hoofs, there was still the Waimauku to be crossed, which meant the water of the small fern, because when the flood waters rose on the islands, only the tops of the cabbage-trees could be seen, like tiny ferns.

Finally, they turned their steps homeward and Shanna forestalled Morgan by announcing that she had prepared lunch earlier. "I thawed out some of grand-mère's incomparable *bouillon* and made coleslaw to go with the cold mutton.''

"Good for you," he said. "I hoped you'd not have forgotten the Kiwi arts, in that lap of luxury you lived in so long."

"What an imagination!" she mocked. "People have such quaint notions about diplomats and trade commissioners and what-have-you. Occasionally girls I went to school with when Dad was in Wellington write to me, usually after they see some picture in the papers of me accompanying Mother and Dad to Buckingham Palace or the Mansion House or something, and they envy me, thinking life is one glorious round of wining and dining.

"In reality we lived as much like here as was possible, except our lamb and fruit and beef and vegetables cost more, even if we made up for a lot in cheaper clothes and household appliances. See, I'm being fair to both Britain and New Zealand! We never lived in serviced apartments, always had a flat or a rented house because we craved family life. So I wasn't likely to forget any of the culinary arts so patiently taught me by my mother and grandmother!"

Clothilde said, twinkling, "This rolls the year away, to be sitting at the table with the children squabbling."

"And Morgan, at least, is old enough to know better," flashed Shanna. "After all, he's practically a generation removed from me. With his mother my grandmother's friend, there's quite a gap."

Morgan gave way to laughter. It was so spontaneous and natural, Shanna experienced a desire to hit him. He sobered, then said mock mournfully, "Yet I recall so distinctly during those exciting days of our sham engagement, your saying most appreciatively that you'd found it much more satisfying to be with an older man."

Her cheeks glowed at the recollection. "Dear me, I must have had softening of the brain, or was I being kind to someone who'd been chivalrous enough to rescue me from an embarrassing situation?"

Morgan took a hasty sip of water. "Damn, I put two

lots of mustard on that bite. No, you were being perfectly sweet and sincere.''

"Wishful thinking," she returned. "Why don't you take mint sauce? Better for your digestion at your age than mustard.''

"Goodness, and here was I concerned about your liver! But maybe it's delayed jet-lag. But it could have been a bit of both.''

"Both what?'' She was genuinely mystified.

"Oh, not liver and jet-lag. I mean sincerity *and* wishful thinking. Sincerity on your part and my wishing you'd always stay as sweet as that. Dan and I are tailing lambs this afternoon—care to join us? Last time you were a great help. Or couldn't you take it now? Just say if you can't. It's mucky at best.''

She looked at him sharply. "Mucky? You don't mean you chop them off now? I don't like—''

"No, of course not. Too much risk of infection. We just slide the rubber rings on as we always did. As you know, in less than half an hour they're frisking round the paddocks as before and all feeling has gone. It's more hygienic and humane in every way. But handling them isn't exactly like picking lavender and mignonette.''

"Don't be ridiculous. I've generations of farmers behind me and only one diplomat. I'll feel I'm really at home if I can come down to the yards. You'll be okay, grand-mère?''

"Of course. I'll be bringing the afternoon tea down at half-past three. I am not yet relegated to uselessness.''

It was marvellous to be working away in the spring sunshine, the smell of wool giving a familiar tang to the air, the mixed sounds of lambs bleating and agitated ewes answering, dogs barking, the feeling of doing a tedious job well. Dan was cheerfully unaware of any undercurrents, and admiring enough of the fact that she'd forgotten none of the technique, to warm Shanna's heart and assist things to become quite blessedly normal.

"How long are you staying, Miss Carew?"

"Make it Shanna, Dan. I'm here for keeps."

She was aware that Morgan had paused with his tool for stretching the ring over the tail. But he let Dan reply to her.

"Oh, that'll sure be good news for the old lady. I thought you were just coming to help out with the hoo-ha for the doings."

"That's what brought me here this early, with Stephanie, but I was already booked for next month to return for good. Then I heard about the reunion."

This time Morgan spoke. "You didn't tell me that, Susannah."

"You didn't ask. We had another month's lease to run on the flat. I thought I'd tie up the ends as soon as they'd left. I didn't want to hustle them out. I'd a few odds and ends of business to tie up. In fact I'd already sent four trunks of stuff off by ship."

"Any particular reason?"

Having Dan Cairns there made it easier. "Just that the folk didn't need me so much and I felt grand-mère did."

Morgan didn't reply. Dan did. "She looks younger already. I guess you need your own folk at that age. Agnes used to go up as often as possible, and Morgan's father and mother, but you are her very own. Which is what she needed."

"I agree," said Morgan Blair. With a direct switch of subject he said, "You'll have more in common with John Forester now he's dabbling in the political scene." (Of course Dan hadn't been at the Vale five years ago, so would think nothing of this). "In fact you could be very useful to him. He has no one to play hostess."

All of a sudden she hated Morgan Blair. He was going to underline for her that if John paid court to her again, it would be for motives of his own. That was despicable. She said smoothly, "I'd be quite pleased to do just that for him, but I hardly see him entertaining often away up here." She picked up another lamb. Her thoughts were

busy. Was Morgan going to try for her again himself?
Oh, not really for her, for Larchwood Vale. With what
pleasure she would turn him down again. Memory of
that other time, five years ago, flooded back to her.

The day she had decided to risk all she wanted from
life on one question, one answer. That farce of an
engagement had gone on long enough. She'd waited and
waited for Morgan to ask her to turn it into reality, to tell
her he found now that he loved her. She couldn't bear it
much longer, the obvious caresses when he thought the
others might notice, the make-believe plans for their
future when someone asked when the wedding was to be,
the unbearable longing she experienced for him to sweep
her into his arms *when they were alone*, to have him tell
her he just *couldn't* give her up.

So she'd said crisply, as they stopped to water their
horses at Gerard's Crossing, standing by their mounts,
"Well, Morgan, I think it's all over, don't you? We've
played our little farce, and now it's time for the curtain.
Thanks immensely for the way you've played up.
Nobody's going to like it, of course. They'll think me
more than fickle—first John, then you. But I've just got to
get away. I can't stand this situation a moment longer.
I'll join mother and dad in Bangkok. Thank heaven for
nomad parents! One can up and off and not have well-
meaning relations and friends trying to patch up what
they'll think is merely a lovers' tiff. We went into it too
suddenly. I hadn't realised how delighted everyone
would be. I could scream every time I hear grand-mère
on the phone telling still someone else that *this* match is
made in heaven! If only they knew!"

Then she had waited. Was it coming, that declaration
she longed for! Morgan had stared down at the ripples
spreading from where the horses were drinking, hadn't
said anything for a tantalising few minutes. He seemed to
be thinking deeply. Then he'd said, "They say the onlookers see most of the game. Mightn't they be right?
Not made in heaven perhaps, but a pretty good match.

Not a sudden burst of trumpets, love at first sight and all that sort of thing, but we've been ... pals ... and ... well, it's time I married and settled down. We've got everything else going for us in the matter of kindred tastes and background and family approval. Why not, Susannah?''

Everything else except the one essential ... love. What a wonderful proposal! Not a cry wrung from him as she'd hoped: "But I love you, I can't bear to let you go out of my life. You've just *got* to marry me!" Oh, no, simply, "Why not, Susannah?"

Her voice had broken with the intensity of her feelings, "Why not? why not? Because I wouldn't go into marriage without even a vestige of real feeling. Because it's not just a case of compatibility and matching tastes, of pleasing the families. Marriage has got to be a complete giving of oneself to the other—a surrender, a total commitment. There's nothing of that between you and me, Morgan, so it's no, no, no!''

There had been another long silence, then he'd said shortly, "Well, you've made yourself plain. You can't do it. So that's it. Gone are the days when people were pressured into marriage. Sorry about that. I'd thought we might have made a go of it, after all.''

Made a go of it. How romantic!

He'd said, "I'll tell the family tonight, my family and your grandmother. Easier that way. You could clear out, go over to Alpenlinden perhaps. You'll have your parents to tell when you join them.''

Later that night when she'd come back from Joy and Lennie's, he'd met her, told her they'd taken it sadly, but accepted it.

Then he'd said, "Come on out for a bit of fresh air for a few minutes.''

She'd known a wild hope. There was a full moon again, a sky blazing with stars, and they'd walked, almost automatically, along the path that led to the larch copse. They'd paused at the far end, where the ground fell away to the plains in a three-sided glade.

He'd said, quite tonelessly, without any real feeling "Perhaps you're right, Susannah. It wouldn't be a marriage that would satisfy you at all. Besides, you're still rather raw from John's defection."

Perhaps that was the moment she should have told him it hadn't been that way at all, that she'd discovered prior to their sudden pretence that she didn't really love John. But Morgan was too astute. He'd have guessed, perhaps, that she'd fallen out of love with John because she'd come up against a greater love. The real thing. That the enforced intimacy of those hours spent on family records had revealed this to her.

And seeing Morgan Hervington-Blair was so tepid about their proposed marriage, she just couldn't take him on those terms. What hell it would be to live with a man and know he didn't love you as you loved him. Far better to part. So the words remained unspoken.

She'd slipped off his ring. It had always been too loose, perhaps an omen that the bond wasn't a close one. It was an emerald, not diamonds. He had said, when they were choosing it for that mockery of an engagement, "It will make you a nice dress ring afterwards!" Now she took his hand, laid it in his palm. Her fingers had trembled with the intensity of longing for a clasp to tighten, for a protest, even now.

He said, "Susannah, I said it was to be yours when we ended this pretence. We've been pals and I'm not likely to give it to anyone else. It matches your green eyes so well, and emeralds are for the month of May, your birth-month. I want you to keep it and wear it whenever you wear green, and remember sometimes that a New Zealand shepherd rather clumsily tried to save from embarrassment a little girl he'd thought a lot of, years ago."

CHAPTER FOUR

There were times in those first few days when Susannah thought she couldn't stand it, that it was too poignant, living under the same roof as Morgan Blair; that some day, in an unguarded moment, she might betray herself, but then life steadied into a routine and she became involved in farm work and the planning for the reunion. Thank goodness it was eight weeks away.

It seemed as if there was going to be a terrific attendance of descendants, and that in itself was revealing. They thought this might be the last for Clothilde, who had heard of those gallant days by word of mouth, who had even shared some of the pioneers' later years when, if they were no longer carving out homesteads from the sod of the plains and the stones of the hills, times had been hard, markets unpredictable, the problems of getting stock to the ports still attended by great natural hazards and the distance from doctors had been a nightmare to women in labour, or when their children suffered accident or illness.

People round here still talked of the Hervington-Blair wife who, in sheer desperation with her two children near choking with diphtheria, saved one by holding him over hot embers sprinkled with sulphur till he coughed up the membranous stuff that was choking him, and two nights later, seeing that method fail with the second, performed a tracheotomy in terror that she might kill the child, but instead had saved her life.

There was the Forester who had broken his leg cutting timber in the bush, had set it himself, passed out with the pain of it, come to, splinted it, and somehow got himself on to his horse and made the homestead.

For light relief there was the story of Victorine's suet dumplings. The rivers on the plains were "braided" ones, with huge spreading shingle beds intersected with many channels twisting in and out of each other, normally safe to ford, but in flood they rose quickly and merged, running bank to bank even, in torrential rain or sudden thaw when the snow washed off the mountains. Most of the time the land between the channels was so dry it grew bushes, even trees, and one or two were permanent islands.

One day a party of young folk crossing from another homestead on horseback were caught by a flash flood due to an electrical storm so far back in the mountains, they had no hint of it. It was a mercy they were not engulfed, but they managed to scramble up the banks and into the centre of the biggest island in the Waimauku. This one was never submerged so at first it was just a lark, and flash floods subsided as quickly as they rose. However, the weather rapidly deteriorated from the south and steady rain set in, keeping the river high.

The horses were all right, cropping the grass, but the young folk were starving by the next day and very cold and wet. There was such a narrow channel between the Waimauku and the homestead that Gerard tried tossing bread across, from a tree that leaned out from the bank, but the gusty wind carried it away. He was more successful with a leg of mutton, well-wrapped, but they needed more than meat as day succeeded day and the rain still fell in torrents.

Then Victorine had her flash of inspiration. She boiled huge suet dumplings, made even more solid by leaving out the rising, and she inserted leeks in one and apples in the other. Clothilde used to recall Gerard telling the tale with great gusts of laughter, because poor Victorine had all a Frenchwoman's flair for light cooking and those dumplings were like cannon-balls. He reckoned his muscles ached for days with the effort of firing them over. But the stranded ones thought them manna from heaven.

They'd built themselves shelters with blown-over trees and rocks and although they were saturated none came to harm. The third day the rain showed signs of abating, the fourth the sun came out and they dried their clothes, the fifth the river went down. But it's to be supposed they never ate another dumpling for the rest of their lives.

Shanna worked steadily on the household chores and filling up the deep freeze with cookies. This fortnight was made easier by the fact John was in Wellington, engaged in some trade negotiations. She felt this had saved her from the rough side of Morgan's tongue. It seemed to her that John's frequent appearances at the homestead in the first week had irked Morgan badly. He'd been civil to him, but only just.

John had taken it quite good-temperedly. Shanna had seen him in a new light. When he talked of political matters he became more animated. She realised, with a twist at her heart, that perhaps this was the direct result of Fran's loss. Perhaps long days spent on the farm gave him too much time for brooding, so he'd plunged into the demanding intricacies of commerce and finance as a sort of bromide.

This night grand-mère retired just before Morgan came in. Shanna didn't know where he'd been. Philip Griffiths was still in Australia, so perhaps he'd been over at Marty's, and that was why he hadn't said where he was going. She pulled herself up—that was stupid.

Morgan didn't have to account for his comings and goings.

"I had a drink and biscuits with grand-mère, but if you've not had anything, Morgan, I'll make you something."

"Oh, good. I'm hungry, as a matter of fact. Any soup left? And how about some cheese and bacon on toast? Be a sport and have some with me. I hate eating alone."

Transient happiness swept over her. This was life as once she had dreamed it might be: Morgan coming home to her at the end of his day at the veterinarian clinic. But in the dream they wouldn't have said goodnight, but gone upstairs to a shared bedroom. It might have been some old house in the Linden Peaks township. She would never, in those early days, have asked him to give up the work he was trained for.

Morgan finished his soup, bit into his savoury toast with relish. "Having you here makes all the difference. Clothilde didn't fancy having a housekeeper, even supposing we could have got one. She would have felt the reins were slipping out of her hands. You can understand that. And we might have got someone who wouldn't have fitted into this atmosphere—either one who wouldn't stop talking, or someone taciturn and moody who didn't talk enough. We managed, with Lois Mains giving us those two days, but some things were slipping."

Warmth pervaded Susannah. Then she told herself she must watch her feelings. How easy it would be to slip into this compromise of knowing she was needed, that she could make life comfortable for the man she loved, because it would be easy to drift into marriage with him. But on his side it would never be a grand passion . . . and she wouldn't settle for less. Imagine lying in a man's arms aware that though he might have a physical need for you, it wasn't true love, that exquisite blend of the spiritual and the flesh; to have to stifle one's own ardor, one's own clamorous need, never to reach the heights, not to hear a man say, in sudden fresh joy, out of the blue, as she had so often heard dad say to mother, "Oh, Marguerite, I *do* love you. I don't know what I did to deserve you." That was what women wanted to be told over and over, not just that a man loved her, but *how* he loved her. Even treating it humorously and having him say, "You *are* a stinker, you mischievous thing, and plague the life out of me, but I *do* love you, heaven help me."

She looked up to find Morgan's eyes fixed on her. She felt the colour rise to her cheeks. He grinned at her, "Do you know, Susannah, you looked then just as you used to look long ago."

She looked down swiftly. "How long ago? Fifteen years, or five?"

She couldn't resist looking up again. The standard light was shining on his smooth fair-to-tawny head and his eyes looked sherry-brown in it.

He grinned. "Five. At the time of our engagement. No, don't correct me . . . at the time of the Big Sham! But I swear that at times you forgot it was sham. That was when you looked like that."

She swallowed. "Well, I wouldn't know myself how I looked."

"Those were the times when I myself couldn't believe it *was* sham. Were you so insensitive to my needs that you didn't realise that? They were comfortable, serene times, Susannah. I thought they might continue. Then all of a sudden you'd come at me with some dirty crack about the impermanence of our relationship. You never stayed serene for long."

She didn't answer, couldn't.

Morgan folded his arms on the table, looking at her searchingly. "Why didn't you stay that way for long?"

Susannah looked reflective, but not evasive, as if the eyes of her mind were turned inward to recapture those moods of five years ago. Then she said, honestly enough, "I think, Morgan, because I felt there was danger in being so comfortable. I think a marriage needs more than that. We'd have reached the heights my parents and your parents have known, know still, I think."

This time Morgan looked away. Then he said, "You thought there was danger in it. What danger, specifically?"

"Because if you felt you'd never reached those heights, never really gone overboard for anyone, perhaps some day, feeling cheated, if someone special came along, you might wish you hadn't settled for something less than the best."

Morgan very carefully adjusted the knitted cosy on the big teapot. Then he said, "Well, that leaves me with nothing to say, doesn't it? A pity."

Suddenly that handsome, square face in front of her looked, oddly, very lean, all planes and angles. It caught Shanna a little off balance. She was used to feeling angry with Morgan Blair, not sorry for him. Had she suddenly made him feel he *was* missing a lot? He wasn't far off forty, and still a bachelor. She said, "Morgan, I'm trying to be honest, and in trying, I think I've hurt you, and believe me, I didn't want to. I was just trying to be analytical about the situation. That *is* how I feel, and I can't help it. I wish I could be otherwise. It would make life here so simple. Everyone would be so pleased, but. . . ."

He nodded, those brown eyes holding the green ones. The look in his was quite tender, even compassionate. He stood up, came to her chair, held out his hands for hers. How warm his hands were! What memories they brought back. Warm hands, well shaped, with hard calluses in the palms.

He took her hands up against his chest, then released them and slipped his arms about her and laid his slightly rough cheek against hers. He said, "Oh, Susannah Carew, thank you for being candid. I find it so hard to see it your way. I always did. It has always seemed a good proposition to me, but it wouldn't satisfy you and I mustn't ask it."

To her surprise, because she'd thought this just a comforting gesture, he put his fingers under her chin, turned her face up to his, smiled down at her with what she thought was brotherly compassion, then kissed her, full on the mouth, in a way that wasn't brotherly at all.

She couldn't move, so stayed there, savouring the sweetness of it, then stirred so that she freed her lips, but he was holding her so tightly that her mouth just trailed across his cheek, and when he held her tighter again, it was buried against his neck beneath his jawbone. She felt him shake a little, knew an answering tremor. He released the intensity of his demanding hold a little so that she could lift her head, lift it to meet a rather quizzical look, one that seemed to insist on an answer so that she was mesmerised into saying, "Yes, what?"

He laughed, little curves each side of his well-cut mouth deepening. "*I* was going to say: 'So what?' to *you*."

She said breathlessly, "What do you mean?"

"Well, wasn't that rather nice? Mightn't we some day, if we gave ourselves a chance, reach those heights? What's the word I want? Something that makes a couple grow together? Oh, I know, propinquity. Nearness. Why don't we try more togetherness instead of hostility, Susannah? They say grand passions expend themselves. Do you have to have sunbursts? Stars wheeling in their courses? Everything in the style of romantic literature?"

She said shakily, and without her usual conviction, "I don't *think* I could settle for less, Morgan."

He noticed the hesitation and drew her closer . . . stridently, the phone rang.

Morgan said, "Oh, hell! Look, must I answer that? Ten to one at this time of night, it's a wrong number. We get very few calls as late as this."

She said, "I think you must. In fact, it could be mother

or father, ringing from Canada, knowing I'm almost bound to be in at this time, nearly midnight. I'll get it.''

She walked over to the desk, said, "Larchwood Vale," and the next moment Marty Griffiths said, "Oh, Shanna, I'm so glad you're still up. Has Morgan gone to bed? Because either I've lost my bag or I've left it in his car. So I wondered if he'd look."

For a recovering moment Susannah stared blankly at the wall in front of her, then she said so naturally she was proud of herself, "Yes, Marty, he's still up. Oh, I do hope it's there. He'll slip out now and find out." She turned. "Marty thinks she may have left her bag in your car. Would you look?"

Morgan went out. Shanna knew she'd be expected to keep talking to Marty till he got back. She said the usual things about how it was always the other things besides money in one's bag that were the bigger loss, and so on.

Marty said, "I know I had it in Timaru because someone asked me for a donation and I wrote a cheque, and I was showing the Whistlers some photos of the children, but I'm blest if I can remember actually having it in the car when Morgan brought me home."

Morgan came in, Shanna turned, said into the phone, "Oh, he's got it. What a blessing! Well, I'll put him on, Marty. Goodnight."

She handed over the receiver to him, and without another word went quietly out of the room and up to bed, where she lay awake a long time with the light out. He tapped on her door, said, "Susannah?" quietly, so not to disturb her grandmother opposite, but she didn't reply. She was noted for dropping into sudden slumber, so he'd think nothing of that.

She would never, never understand Morgan Blair. He just didn't seem able to stay away from Marty. About three o'clock she came to the conclusion that she didn't believe unrequited love ever lived on. It withered away and died for lack of nourishment. She had foolishly fostered her love for Morgan over five lonely years. Now she was going to kill it stone dead. He had some potent charm that disarmed her, made her believe . . . almost . . . that a lukewarm affection was enough for a marriage that would, seemingly, please everyone else and give Morgan Hervington-hyphen-Blair a property every bit as good as the one his sister and her husband were running! He'd come straight back from taking Marty out to try to persuade Clothilde's granddaughter that they could make a good thing out of life together. Philip Griffiths was a fool. Or blind. Shanna sat up, thumped her pillow for the last time, laid her head on it and fell into an exhausted sleep.

It was most annoying that Morgan didn't seem to notice she was being coolly distant the next morning, but it could have been because grand-mère had elected to come down for breakfast.

"I want to hear all about the meeting last night," she said, "and what our branch of the National Party is going to recommend to the government about the price of wheat and the subsidies for fertilisers."

So it had been a meeting and Morgan had taken Marty. Now if Marty had called here for Morgan in the interests of saving petrol by taking just one car, that would have been different, but as this place was considerably nearer Timaru than Ngaio Bend, it was plain ridiculous. Going for Marty and taking her home would give Morgan more time with her. But it didn't matter . . . after all, at exactly three a.m. Susannah Carew had stopped loving Morgan Blair!

The other two talked prices and markets and policies all through the meal. For a woman her age, Clothilde had a surprising grasp of modern trends and wasn't forever talking nostalgically of the old days and comparing them with the new to the disparagement of the latter. But suddenly she said, "You're looking very peaky this morning, *mignonne*. Did you not sleep well?"

"Oh, I slept perfectly," lied Shanna. "In fact, perhaps

too deeply. It works that way sometimes. I could hardly get my eyes open. I won't come outside today, Morgan, I've a fair bit to do inside. I'd like to sort out the jams in the store-room and check the bottled fruit. I thought some of the pears looked doubtful. Once I get outside I don't want to come in.''

Morgan looked disappointed. "I planned on taking you up to Halfway Creek to look at some fencing. You've not been up there yet, and last year we diverted part of the creek across country to irrigate a couple of dad's paddocks.''

"I'll see it another time," said Susannah indifferently. The phone rang. Morgan answered it. "For you, Shanna. A person-to-person call from Wellington. Mr. Forester calling Miss Carew.''

A welcome diversion. John's pleasantly timbred voice said, "Shanna? How are you? No, I don't want you to do anything for me at the Gorge. I've a surprise for you. Guess who's in Wellington for just three days? Mirabel and Donald Stennings from London, on their way to Canberra! They'd love to see you. Said they were in Norway when you left so couldn't say goodbye. I said I was pretty sure I could get you to fly up to see them. How about that? Two hours to get to Harewood. They've got two completely free hours this afternoon. I'd meet you at Rongatai. There's a reception for them tonight, and I could wangle you an invitation. It would mean a lot to them—and to me—to have you there.''

Shanna turned to the two at the table, her eyes sparkling, all peakiness gone. "Grand-mère, two of our dearest friends from London are in Wellington. There's a reception for them tonight, and John would like me to accompany him to it." She just couldn't resist putting it that way. "I have to get the next plane. Would it be all right with you? Just three days.''

"Of course, child. You're a free agent. Waste no time.''

Morgan said dryly, "Sorry I can't run you to Christchurch, but take the Hunter and leave it at the airport. Handy for when you get back. It's too big a slice out of my day otherwise."

But he could go out of his way last night to take Marty to Timaru! Shanna knew that was unfair. That was night-time and the farm work was over. Still ... she ran upstairs singing, "Oh, what a beautiful morning, Oh, what a beautiful day ... " She hoped Morgan got the message.

As she hastily flung her bed together she heard him crossing the brick yard. He was whistling. Whistling what? Suddenly the colour of anger flamed into her face. It was "Whistle and I'll come to ye, my lad." *She* was meant to get a message too.

She came downstairs in an elegant green suit with white facings and gold-chain trim, emerald green patent shoes and handbag. Grand-mère looked approving. "You inherited your mother's dress sense. Even in those abominable dungarees you wear in the yards, you achieve style."

Shanna burst out laughing. "You absurd darling! You know very well that in the pens I'm just the grubby little Shanna I was at twelve. Now, behave while I'm away. I hate to leave you, but I'd love to see the Stennings."

Morgan had the Hunter waiting for her, engine running. The sun shone on him so brilliantly it lit up the fair streaks in his hair. Even his brows had bleached hairs in them, and his lashes. She felt the old fascination stirring within her and clamped down on it.

He opened the back door, put her white hide case in, and opened the driver's door for her. She got in. He leaned in through the open window, said quite simply, "I wish you weren't going, Susannah. I thought last night we were nearer an understanding than we've ever been. Don't let this break make a difference."

She blinked a little as if she didn't know what he was getting at. "Oh, that. Don't read too much into it. Just a mood of the moment, Morgan. Things look different in daylight."

His mouth twisted wryly—chagrin, she supposed. He said, "All things? This, for instance?" and his head came farther in and he laid his mouth very deliberately and possessively on hers. She couldn't move away because he'd made the seat-belt a little too tight for her. He lifted his face two inches from hers and the brown eyes danced with merriment. "These compulsory seat-belt regulations have their advantages."

Susannah lost her iciness. "Oh, go away, Morgan Blair!" she said, and revved up the engine a little.

He said deliberately, "Don't get carried away these few days in Wellington. John Forester can't give you your heart's desire . . . to remain here."

She was startled. "Why not? I mean, he's just next door. Though. . . ."

"We heard a whisper at the meeting last night that he may stand at the next election."

"But that wouldn't mean he left here. None of the members who have farms give them up. It's too precarious a livelihood, especially in New Zealand with an election every three years. He has a good couple on the farm and a splendid farm cadet. And air travel makes it so easy."

"I've reason to believe he can't carry on much longer. He's mortgaged up to the hilt. He's lived it up a bit since Fran died. Pity there isn't more than one son. Another one might have been a better farmer. John's heart isn't in it. So bear that in mind. It mightn't be as ideal as it might seem."

"What a prosaic view you take, Morgan! Wives follow their husbands. They don't marry them for a way of life—or ought not to. Besides, I'm not an impulsive twenty-two-year-old now. I've got no stardust in my eyes. I'm merely off to meet old, dear friends. But if I happen to enjoy myself with John while so doing, it has nothing whatever to do with you, Morgan. Stand clear . . . my steed is fretting at the bit." She let in the clutch and moved off.

It took her most of the journey to Christchurch to recover her poise. Nothing seemed the same as of yore. The Blairs were retiring to Linden Peaks township soon, and Stephanie and Brent Morley would be moving into the homestead. Morgan was managing Larchwood Vale for Clothilde. How much better if another manager had been in charge; and soon Forester Gorge might pass into alien hands. No wonder Grand-mère wanted a last reunion. After that . . . the deluge!

How could John consider giving up the Gorge? Had he lost heart when he lost Fran? Would it make a difference if he married again? If he knew that in time he might have sons to carry on his name in the place where his ancestors had made a wilderness of tussock and boulder into a rich, productive estate? Rich no longer, seemingly. Of course farming, of late, with such changes in world markets, inflation, and natural disasters, had been anything but steady. Nevertheless Morgan had kept Larchwood on an even keel. Could it be true that John had lived it up since Fran died? Or was that what Morgan wanted her to believe?

As soon as she was airborne, an element so familiar to her, her spirits began to rise, and in no time they were dropping down over Wellington. There, first in the line, was the familiar figure of John, dark-suited, nothing but his tanned face distinguishing him from any other city business man. She felt as if the clock slipped back because he had no hesitation. He simply held out his hands, took her face between them, kissed her.

"This is magnificent, darling," he said. "I can't believe my incredible luck. Thank God for air-travel! Last night I felt as flat as a pancake—too many meetings, too many people, too much grind. Then the Stennings happened along. They asked where I lived, twigged it was the area you came from, and asked if I knew you."

He grinned, "I nearly said, 'Know her . . . I almost married her.' Instead I said, My homestead is next to her grandmother's. Would you like me to get her here?"

She was starry-eyed. "I just love the Stennings. When my mother was so ill, Mirabel was magnificent. She used to be a nursing Sister and took many a nightwatch with us. Donald was great too; he used to take Dad out for long walks."

John had her by the arm, steering her along the covered in ramp towards the terminal waiting-room area. He said, a note of surprise in his voice, "I didn't know your mother had had a severe illness. How come I missed out on that bit of news?"

"We never let grand-mère know. We thought she would have insisted on flying over and it could have been too much for her. She isn't to know yet, John, till Mother gets here for the reunion and grand-mère can see for herself there's nothing to fear. That's why we've not been home for so long. It must have seemed callous to her that at this stage of her life we stayed away longer."

They were into the foyer by now, waiting the luggage call. John stopped and faced her, with dark, almost black eyes on hers. "She thought you had another reason that you didn't dare come back. Said she thought it would be too poignant for you; that at Larchwood Vale you'd experienced things that had left scars. I couldn't help but hope it meant you'd regretted you'd ever given me up. That was when I made up my mind if I had a chance to go to Britain, I'd take it. Then I heard you were coming home."

Shanna said, "John, how did grand-mère come to tell you this? In what exact circumstances?"

"When she had an attack of bronchitis this winter. Morgan was in a foul mood and said you ought to be here even if your mother couldn't be. Grand-mère took him up rather sharply. You know that way of hers, like a tigress defending her young. She wouldn't hear any criticism of you. She said, as far as I can remember, 'Shanna is so vulnerable, so warm-hearted, she cannot trust herself to return. She is afraid she might repeat her youthful folly all over again. And she has her pride. Pride is such a formidable thing in the young.' So I pulled a few strings and thought I would come to see you. Instead, you came to me. Shanna, I know this is no place . . . clean in the middle of a busy airport . . . but we may not have much more time alone together . . . oh, hell! Look who's coming! The minister of agriculture. He's important to me, so I can't pretend not to see him and hustle off with you.''

But she was glad of the interruption. John was going too fast. She was interested in meeting the minister. Her father had spoken of him often.

The call came over for collection of luggage; they went to get it, piled into John's departmental car, and in the thick of Wellington traffic, personal conversation took a back seat.

It was a delight to meet Mirabel and Donald again. At the reception she met many people with whom they'd had contact in London, apart from the Prime Minister and the Leader of the Opposition, and a former High Commissioner whom she'd liked very much even if he hadn't belonged to the party she herself favoured. John watched her with appreciative eyes.

He came up to the Stennings' apartment with them afterwards to share a last cup of tea and sandwiches. Then he took Shanna to her room on the floor below. He said, smilingly, "I can find it in me to be glad the Stennings are off to Canberra in thirty-six hours, and that you're going to stay on till I fly home this weekend. We might even be able to take up that interrupted conversation before then.''

She nodded, but said quite mildly, "But it won't lead anywhere . . . I don't want to be involved with anyone, thanks. Just to enjoy being home.''

He went to say something, checked himself, then said, "Well, I can bide my time, I suppose. Goodnight, my dear.''

The turning of her cheek was instinctive. He kissed her lightly, and said with a grin in which she saw the old

John she had fancied long ago, "Well, that'll be enough to go on with, but don't think you'll always get away with a peck. Goodnight."

Shanna went into her room, gazed into space, sitting on the bed. The evening had been very pleasant, a world she knew so well ... but hundreds of miles down south, against the mountains, was all that comprised her true world ... all she loved.

CHAPTER FIVE

Shanna found to her surprise that she enjoyed the rest of the time. Wellington was in its most sparkling mood, when the cruel winds lay dormant and the gorse-blossom on the tops of the hills and the fans of tree-ferns in the gulleys mocked the high-rise buildings and the cosmopolitan air of the capital as if to say nature couldn't be hidden altogether under great monuments of concrete and glass. The sun caught the white sails of yachts tacking to and fro, sparkled on the remnants of snow on the Rimutakas across the harbour, which lay like a cobalt pool beneath the matching blue of the cloudless sky.

This, after all, was the world she had known most of her life, in diplomatic circles, and in spite of her conviction that she was essentially a child of the soil there was a verve and stimulation about this. Maybe she had enough of her father in her, after all, to enjoy it. Impossible not to be flattered at being asked at short notice to various functions, having her opinion asked on certain matters, even being interviewed on TV about being secretary to a father involved in trade missions and knowing the international scene.

When they flew into Harewood they would have to make their way home separately as John also had his car parked there. Shanna was sorry, because some perversity made her feel she'd like to be delivered home by John. But they were paged on arrival and John was told someone had backed into his car only that morning and it had been taken to a workshop for de-denting.

"I can run you up for it next week, John," she offered. "Good thing I was here."

They headed out of the city. "We'll lunch at the White House at the Selwyn Crossing," said John. "Are you in a hurry to get home?"

"No, why?"

"I meant to call on the Lovells at Mata Flat. He couldn't get to the Wheat Board meeting and I said I'd report to him. They're out towards the coast from Rakaia. Marvellous place—once all swampy like Longbeach, and drained in the same way, in the early days. Its wonderfully fertile."

They came over the Selwyn Bridge, slowed to go into the White House parking-space and were passed by a station-wagon. Neither occupant saw them as they were both glancing towards the river-bed, perhaps to see if the Californian poppies that covered it were beginning to bloom, but John and Shanna certainly saw *them*! Morgan, dressed for the city, and beside him a woman with copper-bright hair, dressed in an elegant blue suit that would match her eyes. Marty Griffiths! Shanna caught her breath and was cross with herself for betraying her feelings. John snorted. "There he goes, off with the glamorous Marty and Philip safely across the Tasman, poor beggar."

Shanna said nothing; she couldn't. John said "Sorry to sound so self-righteous, but that fellow gets my goat at times. Most chaps, turned down by a girl, take it on the chin and find someone else, like I did. But Morgan still dangles after Marty."

Shanna found herself saying, "It's so hard to believe,

of either Morgan or Marty. Morgan was so straight in his
dealing all those years ago when we were youngsters.
And in his farm management his integrity is unquestion-
able. Everything is audited and accounted for, and he's
certainly made it pay even through the flunctuations of
the last few years."

John hesitated, then said, "A chap hates to decry
another fellow, Shanna, especially some ne he's known
all his life, but. . . ."

Shanna said, "Go on. It's not fair to stop there. Put me
in the picture, John."

He parked, loosened his belt, said, "I think I should,
for your sake and your mother's."

She was startled. "For mother's? You mean as chief
heir to grand-mères estate? John, I'd never believe any
skulduggery on Morgan's part."

"I know I don't mean he'd cook the books, or anything
like that, but it's not natural for any man just drawing
wages to work some sort of agreement so that he gets a
share in the estate. Keep a tight watch on things, Shanna.
If your grandmother's solicitor, who also happens to be
Morgan Blair's, comes out insist on being present to
watch your mother's interests. I expect she'll turn some
of her shares over to you, rather than just leave them to
you, but I'd like to think it was all there to be turned over.
There, I've said enough to put you on your guard. Let's
forget Morgan Blair and just enjoy ourselves."

Susannah tried to push the matter to the back of her
mind. She dared not flare up in Morgan's defence, but
she was sure it was ungrounded. The matter of his being
out with Marty was harder to dismiss. They had an
excellent lunch—if only Shanna had felt like eating—then
they were on their way to Mata Flat.

It was fine homestead and the Lovells were charming.
Shanna thought Mrs. Lovell's eyes rested on her
speculatively once or twice, and from her to John. While
the men talked, the two women walked around the
garden, cherished and tended by Mrs. Lovell, and talked

of the children away at boarding-school, then came back for afternoon tea.

On the way home, John still driving the Hunter, she decided on a little probing of her own. But she must take care to do it so he had no idea who had instilled the doubts in her mind. In fact she mustn't let him know she had any doubts at all.

He wasn't a bit evasive. She watched his lean, handsome face for signs. The talk at Lovells' helped to make it easy to introduce. They had discussed prices of grain and wool, of subsidies and costs and the state of the world's markets as affecting exports. So she was able to say quite naturally "How have you fared at the Gorge, John, through difficult years?"

"Not too well, Shanna, as a matter of fact. No one's found it easy, of course. The boom years of the nineteen fifties that my father knew are long behind us, but I could have made out much better had I just had the run-of-the-mill ups and downs other farmers experienced."

"What do you mean, John? Or shouldn't I ask?"

"I think you, of anyone, should know. I had a serious setback. I won't go into details, but in short, with the idea of consolidating my position, and in turn providing a certain protection for my son, or sons, if I was lucky enough to have any, a protection that wouldn't rely solely upon the the vagaries of farming, I invested some capital—not wisely, though I couldn't have forseen that. I, like many others, lost the lot. Later, Fran was ill, and it was pretty expensive. I wanted the very best treatment for her. Social Security covered very little of it. Then we had that disastrous flood. Oh, there was some compensation, but it still affected returns. So for the first time for years, Forester Gorge is heavily mortgaged. But it'll come right, I'm keeping my head above water. I'm not letting it worry me. I've been wanting to tell you for some time, only I haven't found the right moment till now. I didn't want you labouring under any false impressions— it's not fair to a woman."

Shanna was at a loss. All her instincts were to comfort him. Oh it was hellish being a woman. One's best intention could so easily be misconstrued.

She said, finally, "John, I've an idea that five years ago I messed up your life and Morgan's rather badly. It was such a tangle. I don't trust my judgment any more ... I just want to be with grand-mère. I'm sorry the Gorge is a burden to you, but our forefathers weathered out worse times than these. They had huge mortgages too and came through. When the reunion is over I may be able to think through some of my own problems. Till then, just let us all be friends, for grand-mère's sake."

He patted her knee. "Okay, pal. I feel safer about you now I've uttered that word of caution about Morgan. You can't blame me, can you? You fell for him in a big way five years ago and put paid to my increasing hopes that you might marry me. But now you're older and wiser, so ... don't let your feelings run away with you. Oh, I hate like hell your living the same house with him."

Shanna managed a laugh. "That doesn't mean a thing! We're at loggerheads most of the time. He despises me for not coming home sooner to grand-mère and he made me so flaming mad I didn't tell him why. All I care about is being with her I don't want to get involved with anyone emotionally. Ah, we're nearly at your place. I won't come in when you get out. Grand-mère may have found it a long day on her own."

She was surprised, when she turned into the courtuard at the Vale, to find the station-wagon standing there, and still more to see two small cases outside it and two schooltype mackintoshes draped over them. Even if they'd spent some time at Mata Flat, Morgan and Marty couldn't have had long to Christchurch or wherever they'd been going. But who on earth did these belong to?

As she reached the back door two figures dashed out headlong, feminine ones. No mistaking their identity with those two copperheads: Marty's daughters They'd been seven and five last time she'd seen them, so they were twelve and ten now—Dorothy and Roberta.

Dorothy gasped out, "Morgan told us to go back for the cases and we forgot and heard you coming and thought you might run over them. Did you? Oh, no you didn't. Hullo, Susannah, it's a long time since we've seen you."

Shanna laughed. "Nearly everyone calls me Shanna for short. Susannah is such a mouthful. Hullo, girls."

Roberta said, "O, Morgan never calls you Shanna when he talks about you to mum, so we think of you as Susannah. Say, what a gorgeous suit you're wearing. Paris, I suppose?"

Shanna chuckled. "No, my lamb, London. How come you're here? I saw. . . ." Better not to say she'd seen their mother with Morgan heading for the city.

The girls didn't notice and rushed on. "We're staying here, and Richie and Peter are with Graham and Rhona, our married couple. So they can help Graham on the farm after school, you see. There's so much to see to at this time of year. But Morgan said he could cope with us because you're here. Anyway we're very domesticated, mum saw to that. Said you can get by in life without a lot of accomplishments like playing the harp or tossing the caber, or being able to paint or weave, but every woman ought to be proficient at dish-washing and baking and scrubbing floors and things. So you don't mind, do you, Susannah? We'll try not to talk you to death, because we promised Morgan that, but we rather hope you like to talk too!"

She blinked a bit. "Oh, I do. I mean I like to talk, and I don't mind your being here a bit. I'd love female company, especially if you're gigglers, but—"

"Oh, we are. Dad says he doesn't know what he's done to deserve three hopeless gigglers like us and mum. He call us his gaggle of gigglers. I'm glad you're a giggler. We do hate people who don't see the funny side of things. It's so ghastly to make a joke and not have people rolling in the aisles.''

Susannah said solemnly, "If there's one thing I'm really good at, it's rolling in the aisles In fact, even when there are no aisles within twenty miles, I roll just the same, but tell me—"

Again her query as to why they were there was drowned out because the girls considered this a prince of jokes. Suddenly Morgan's head and Morgan's voice appeared in the doorway. "It's no good, Susannah, you'll never be answered. They're here because right this minute, Marty is flying over the Tasman Sea to join Philip. His time has been extended. I was over there when he rang. So much for my day up at the irrigation channel! Graham rang to say one of the stud ewes was in trouble. We'd fixed it up and were having morning tea when Philip rang.

"The doings have been extended to include a four-day tour of the Great Barrier Reef—chance of a lifetime. Those two never get away by themselves. Marty flapped, of course, in the way you women do . . . said she couldn't possibly, she had a huge pile of washing and the girls had dental appointments in Ashburton this week, and someone was coming to tea tomorrow, and she had to pass a vote of thanks at the Women's Division in the township . . . I've never known men to feel as indispensable as women do. I grabbed the phone from her, said, It's okay, Phil, she *can* make it. I'll see she does, I'll get her on the next available flight and ring you from Harewood what time to meet her. And I did.

"I brought the washing over here when I picked the girls up from the school bus. Marty and Phil have had only one holiday on their own the whole time they've been married, and just look at those two . . . anybody'd be glad to get away from them occasionally!''

The little one, Roberta, turned around and gave Morgan a big hug. "I do love you Morgan. This is going to be fun. I only just remember you when you were here before, Susannah, but we've heard a lot about you from Morgan. And mum says you're the most beautiful thing she's seen. Morgan, can we go and groom the ponies now?''

"You can not. Leave that till tomorrow after school. Susannah's just got in after a flight and a long drive, and she must be tired. Take your things up and I'll give you some sheets and pillow-cases and you can make up your beds, then come on down and set the table for us. I've got some T-bone steaks, Susannah. I rather fancy myself at the grilling, and we'll just have rolls and salad with it, and bottled greengages and cream to follow. Right, girls, get those cases. Have a good time in Wellington, Susannah?''

She felt odd. All the way from Selwyn she had hardened her heart against this Morgan Blair who surely was philandering with a man's wife, in his absence . . . and now he was here, being most avuncular with her little daughters, and he'd bundled the wife off for a second honeymoon with her husband in Australia! Talk about unpredictable males! She didn't know what to believe about either John Forester or Morgan Blair! And Marty actually thought she, Susannah Carew, was beautiful! How strange.

Morgan had cast the first doubts when he'd mentioned Fran's unhappiness. That had been explained away as homesickness. He'd been doubtful about John's financial position. But surely anyone could make a bad investment, have a run of poor luck, and at the same time find himself inpoverished by his wife's illness? So she had thought the less of Morgan for seemingly exaggerating the position.

But then John had been so ready to believe the worst of Morgan when they'd seen him with Marty. (Hadn't you too? her conscience niggled at her!) Well, in fairness to Morgan she must see John knew why they'd been together. But she mustn't appear to be leaping to Morgan's defence. She hated this rivalry between the two men. She was also very dubious about their motives. She must try to get John over here while the Griffiths girls were here. He'd be bound to ask why. But she didn't need to try. He came over that night.

They were just settling down with after-dinner coffee. He tapped at the back door, called out, "It's only me," came to the back of Shanna's low chair dropped a kiss on the top of her head and said, "Thought you might wonder where this had got to," and dropped a silver mesh purse into her lap. "You slipped it into my pocket at the Llewellyns' reception last night when Gwen asked you to help her serve a round of drinks."

Shanna thanked him, and John said, "Hullo girls, what are you doing here? Got to the age of paying evening calls on your own, have you?"

"No fear," said Dorothy. "We're staying for five or six nights. Morgan rushed mum off to join dad on a trip round the Great Barrier Reef. Wish we could have gone too . . . they go out in glass-bottomed boats to see the fish and the coral. But when we said this, Morgan said even if there'd been time to get us all there, that wasn't the right idea at all. This is a second honeymoon for them. How many honeymoons can you have, anyway? I thought there was just one, straight after the wedding."

Morgan laughed. "Technically that's all, Doro. It's just a term for a holiday when two people can get away by themselves, and—er—recapture a bit of the atmosphere of their honeymoon."

"Oh, is that what it is? Thanks for explaining it. It's nice not to be hushed down by grown-ups and told you wouldn't understand. Because how else can you find out, except by asking, yet some people say children should be seen and not heard."

Morgan twinkled. "That's a fallacy, if ever there's one! I've never yet met any children who could be seen and not heard. And heard very loudly! But after this coffee you two must do your homework and you can watch your two favourite programmes, then bed. Time was when we could set a bedtime for kids, but not now. I asked your mother exactly what you're allowed to watch each night they'll be away, so no trying to con me into staying up later.''

Roberta said quickly, "Mrs. Larchwood said she'd teach me how to do tapestry work while we were here."

"I did," said Clothilde, "but the thing I did not say was when, and naturally, with so much coming and going, we are later tonight. Morgan won't want a late night either, because with giving up so much time, first with the sick ewe at Ngaio Bend, then rushing your mother to the airport, he has a big day tomorrow, catching up."

That tidied that up nicely, thought Shanna gratefully. In bed, on the verge of sleep, she decided she was tired of those two men behaving like that about each other. Stupid things! Because she was no longer interested in either of them. Pity some personable man wouldn't dawn on the Larchwood horizon, some third man who might fire her interest, once and for all, and prove to her that her world ought never to have been bounded by only John Forester and Morgan Blair.

She had no idea that that third man was at that very moment in Christchurch intent upon getting to Larchwood Vale the next day!

CHAPTER SIX

Even though she'd set her alarm half an hour early to cope with getting two lunches and seeing the girls off in time for the school bus, as she went to shower she heard them talking to her grandmother. She emerged in her dressing-gown and went in.

She cocked a reproving eye at the girls. "Don't you know my grandmother needs a little extra beauty sleep at her age? I don't think you'd better make a habit of this."

Dorothy said, gazing in admiration at the petal-soft cheeks and blue eyes, "She doesn't need beauty sleep; besides I think she just loves having us here."

"Indeed, but that is so," said old Clothilde. "No need to fuss, Susannah. I'm waited on as it is, with breakfast in bed every morning, and this is like a tonic. It takes me back to the days when three children came to roost on our bed every morning. It spells happiness to me. No, Susannah, don't turn away to hide your emotion . . . the sadness goes out of old griefs year by year as one grows older, till only the remembrance of the happiness we knew together is left. I woke to the sound of children's voices coming from that room, and for a drowsy moment

I thought it was Gerard and Lucien plotting mischief together, so I called out to the girls to come in.

"Come and sit down too, child, before the rush of the day is upon you. I always gave thanks for those waking moments . . . to see the sun peeping over the tops of Hervington-Blair's pines a mile away, and beyond that, the glitter of snow on the far ranges, before household duties demanded one stay inside."

Susannah stayed a moment or two, then left the girls to it. She wouldn't rob Clothilde of the company she'd lacked too long How blind could one be ? She'd crept downstairs every morning so her grandmother could slumber on.

She sped downstairs and began pouring out orange juice and shaking out cornflakes, since the girls spurned porridge. Morgan joined her, got out grand-mère's tray, and as always put a flower in a tiny vase. "My Disraeli touch," he'd said laughingly on Shanna's first morning. Today it was one of the miniature daffodils from Clothilde's rock-garden. Yesterday it had been a spray of the pink saxifrage, the day before, forget-me-nots.

No doubt John would have said Morgan had an ulterior motive. Oh, dear, she was back to thinking about those two men again! The girls clattered downstairs. Morgan would take them a mile to the crossroads where the Linden Peaks school bus would pick them up with half a dozen others.

She sorted out the washing, switched on the automatic machine. Lovely to hang clothes out on the lawn in the back garden, in the air redolent with violets and freesias, pure with the clarity of alpine breezes. How much better than the steamy launderettes and tumbler-driers in London . . . though they'd been immensely grateful for them. She said so to Morgan.

"It must be. I ought to have apologised to you for dumping all that washing on you, but I knew you'd cope. Marty was horrified. But I said, 'Oh, shucks, she's a Larchwood after all; that cosmopolitan veneer is just that, skin-deep and no more. Given a late snowstorm and the power cut off and lambs to be mothered Susannah would revert to the resourcefulness of Victorine Rose. A washing and ironing like this will be nothing to her.' But I'll wash the dishes for you."

"I won't turn that down, ' said Susannah, warmth at her heart because he'd talked of her like that to Marty. She recalled what the girls had said. Did he often talk of her to Marty? Suddenly it was all glorious fun, life as it was meant to be lived, and well-balanced ... age looked after in comfort and love ... children sitting on a grandmother's bed, being listened to, and listening, soaking up the wisdom that came with years of living; a family atmosphere at breakfast, a sharing of the chores, a man to cook for, wash for, sew his buttons on, help him at sheep-yards and cattle-pens.

After Morgan had gone on his rounds of the sheep-dotted downs, old Clothilde smiled to herself as she heard her granddaughter singing about her household tasks. She drifted off to sleep again.

Dan came in for his lunch, too. Agnes was taking her turn at aiding the play-centre at Linden Peaks today. He said to the fish Susannah had concocted from a tin of smoked *terakihi* fillets, "It makes all the difference to the place, having you here, on days like this. Besides the boss has more time to spend outside now, so we've got an enormous lot of the extra jobs done. Last year all we could do was concentrate on the stock, apart from doing that spot of irrigation. It was such a success."

Clothilde twinkled. "They're too nice to say so, *cherie*, but what they mean is they can now both stay away for hours at a time. Oh, but I saw through all those excuses for returning to the house ... they'd run out of fencing wire, they'd forgotten to take the wire-strainer with them, they had a phone call to put through ... I appreciated it all while deploring the necessity. I think we're looking on you in the nature of a godsend." ·

"We are," said Morgan, and fleetingly his eyes met Susannah's.

Dan added, "And a godsend done up in a very glam wrapping too . . . I'm one of the men who prefer blondes. That's why I picked my Agnes."

Shanna gave a disparaging tweak at her shoulder-length blocks. "It's not blonde. It's just tow."

Dan said, "What utter rubbish! It was never tow. It was honey-coloured. Dark honey. *Rewarewa* honey."

"I still call it tow," said Shanna, "and against that lovely copper of the girls' heads this morning, it must have looked really washed out."

"I can never understand women," said Dan, passing his plate for a second helping. "Nessie, now, likes raven locks. She even talked seriously of dyeing hers, so for once I put my foot down."

"How?" queried Morgan, with interest.

"I said if she dared, I'd feel I'd fallen for her under false pretences, and I'd lose all interest in her and start chasing after the very next blonde to cross my path." They laughed. Dan added, "It's a lot of nonsense, though. You fall for the person, not the colouring or the looks. Look at Phil Griffiths. He couldn't stand redheaded women—with good reason—yet he married Marty. And women are supposed to fall for the tall, dark, handsome types. Good job they all don't, or some of us would be out on a limb."

Susannah spoke before she thought. "I can't understand how that idea ever took on. I much prefer them fair and broad. Bother the height and the dark hair." Next moment she felt her cheeks warm. She was aware that Morgan looked at her sharply and she turned away hastily to ask Clothilde to pass the jam. Her grandmother was looking impishly amused.

Morgan said easily enough, "Dan and I should get up and bow, though after a meal like that it will be hard to get up, anyway. Susannah, we won't be back for afternoon tea. We'll take a flask and scones. That'll give us a full afternoon with no interruptions. Okay? The chap who helps Brent is going to bring the girls back from the bus when he picks up his youngsters."

Susannah put a casserole of hogget chops in the oven, made an apple crumble, and scrubbed potatoes ready to put in the oven later. That left her free to tackle the ironing. Clothilde sat in the kitchen, talking to her, and attaching silk patches to one of her exquisite quilts. Susannah felt a wave of love for her grandmother sweep over her. Oh, grant she had many years yet.

At four all was finished, so she made herself and Clothilde some tea and they retired to a little room at the back of the house that caught the westering sun beautifully at this time of day. It was always called the Shakespeare room because when Clothilde was a bride here, in the long evening that knew neither radio nor television, she had embroidered a miniature set of pictures of all the herbs and flowers mentioned in his plays and sonnets.

It had comfortable old wing chairs with pastel-tinted chintz covers, basket chairs, low bookshelves against the walls with long-loved volumes of poetry, novels old and new, dominoes, checkers, a chessboard, Clothilde's work-basket beside her favourite chair. Presently, in the sun, Clothilde dozed.

There was a ring at the front door. Callers hardly ever used it; mostly they continued around the drive to the back door. As Shanna reached a side passage, she saw a taxi being driven away. Good lord, they weren't expecting overnight visitors! How odd. The taxi must have come right from Linden Peaks.

She opened the door to a dark-haired man, in a light-weight suit that suggested the tropics; he had an extremely expensive-looking case in his hand and the faintest hint of a foreign air. She lifted her eyes to search his face, came to the conclusion she wasn't dreaming, and said gladly, "Oh, Louis! My cousin Louis! How

absolutely marvellous. I'd have recognized you anywhere. Oh, do come in."

There was the faintest hesitation. Then he stepped in,
said, "Fancy you're recognising me after all these
years," and kissed her.

"Oh, this is fabulous, Louis. Did you hear about the
reunion? Did grand-mère write and tell you? Perhaps
she wanted to surprise me, and didn't say."

"Reunion? No ... had no idea one was coming
up...."

"No wonder you're surprised. It's only five years since
the last one, but she feels the years are catching up on
her, and decided one should take place now. Oh, I do
hope you can stay for it. Please don't say it's a fleeting
visit. It's not far off. You saw practically nothing of New
Zealand fifteen years ago. You must tour around this
time, making this your headquarters, perhaps. And of
course the next time you couldn't make it, and only
Françiose came. Oh, if only she were here! But I mustn't
speak of sad things as soo as you arrive. How long are
you here for?"

Again the slight hesitation. Then he smiled and said,
"I really don't have to hurry back to Tahiti. I'm very
much my own master. I've a competent staff back there. I
had business in Auckland and Wellington, and didn't
ring to say I was coming as I wanted it to be a surprise
How wonderful your grand-mère is still alive."

"Just leave your bag there," said Susannah. "I'll get a
room ready for you quite soon. We've two of the
Griffiths girls staying. I think you might recall their
mother. She was Marty Reddington then, fresh from
England and helping Joy and Lennie Logie at Alpenlinden. Morgan was dating her a bit. He was a vet then; now
he's manager here. But Marty married Philip Griffiths.
They're in Australia at the moment, so we're looking
after their girls. The boys are with the married couple on
their farm. But come in to grand-mère. Let's see if she
recognises you too."

"Don't be disappointed if she doesn't," said Louis. "Old people's faculties fail. I was surprised you did, after so long."

"Well, apart from all this sartorial elegance, you're certainly still my cousin Louis Rossignol. What fun we had! Come on."

Her grandmother knew him immediately, and held out her hands. There was a suggestion of the Frenchman about him as he kissed first her hand, then both cheeks. "Madame!" he said.

"You'd better make it Tante Clothilde as you did before, even if it is to the Rossignols you claim kinship. Oh, but it has been such a long time, and you have been such a poor letter-writer. We had thought when your sister came to live here we might see you again, but of course," her voice trembled and her eyes misted, "Françoise was here with us so short a time; and it was so sad for you, Louis, that you did not know for so long because you were on that expedition in South America and couldn't be reached. You were being brought out, injured, even then. Tell me, Louis, are you climbing again?"

"No, tante, not climbing. I'm devoting myself to business these days. That's why I'm here. I had to visit an agency in Auckland, then come to Wellington unexpectedly, and couldn't resist coming on down here. Not that I tried to resist, of course. Oh, no, I thought I might be able to recapture a little of that long-ago vacation, but I had not dared hope it would be so felicitous an occasion and that my cousin would be here. Last I heard she was in Zurich, and then London."

Shanna was surprised. "You heard? But there's been this lack of correspondence. . . ."

"Your *papa* is well enough known to occasionally be mentioned in the papers—the American papers, and I'm often in Los Angeles. But this is delightful, your being here. For how long?"

"For the rest of my life, I hope."

There was a flicker in the warm brown eyes. Louis had always been quick on the uptake. He would substitute for that ... the rest of her grandmother's life. But Shanna knew she was home for good.

She went off to brew Louis some coffee and brought back some petits-fours with it. Oh, but the engaging youngster of fifteen years earlier had grown into a very personable man. He said, "I've been getting Tante Clothilde to put me in the picture ... tell me who is here and what they do. She says Morgan has never married. Did he pine after the Marty you mentioned? Perhaps one of these one-woman men one reads of but never meets, *hein*?"

Shanna left it to Clothilde to answer. "Indeed no. That was but a passing fancy. Marty had already fallen for Philip Griffiths before she came here. He was a temporary liaison officer on an immigrant ship. But why am I telling you this? You would remember Philip, of course?"

Louis looked puzzled. "I can't say I do. I recall Marty vaguely. Perhaps this Philip made less impression."

Susannah and her grandmother burst out laughing. Louis looked puzzled. "He ought to have made more of an impression on you literally, Louis," giggled Susannah. "He was the one who rescued you from that willow by the brook when you couldn't get down. The branch broke before he got up to you, and in trying to grab you, he cascaded down after you and winded you completely."

"Oh, that chap, of course! You know, it's the oddest thing, I got such a crack on the head in that accident that my memory is appalling, though some things are quite clear. The most stupid things evade me." He turned to Shanna. "I remember the time Morgan chastised us for taking out that leaky boat. That makes him a lot older than us, doesn't it, but perhaps it was only that we were so young."

"He's ten years older than you, eleven years older than

me," said Shanna. "He seemed very adult then, because he had authority over us, but suddenly one grows up to one's seniors and the years cease to matter."

"That's good," said Morgan's voice from the doorway, "or else I should feel a Methuselah. Hullo, Louis, how good to see you. But where did you spring from?"

"From Harewood as far as today is concerned, but in the first place I flew in to Auckland from Tahiti on business. It's only eight hours from Tahiti. How strange that till now I've not come to see you all again; why I didn't come to recapture the happiness of that youthful holiday, I'll never know."

Morgan sat down. "Perhaps it was understandable, as so much sadness has come since, so much water flowed under the bridges. Have you revived your father's business, Louis? How good if that's so. He had a most unfortunate time from what we could gather from Françoise. A man of such integrity to be caught up in such skulduggery and to wear himself out repaying people whom his business associates cheated. It reminded me of Sir Walter Scott, writing himself to death to repay those who had suffered through the failure of the publishing business he'd engaged in."

Louis said, "Thank you, Morgan. Yes, that was it. Though had my mother still been alive, he might have made it without ruining his health. He was within sight of clearing up the debt of honour and his insurance cleared it all up. It left me without a penny, of course, but I'm on top of it now. No, not the same business. I thought it better to start out on my own. I deal in textiles—the fabulous Tahitian fabrics."

At that moment the girls rushed in, kissed Morgan first because he was nearest the door, then, as they went over to Clothilde and Shanna, checked as a handsome stranger rose from the depths of the big chair and bowed to them.

"Greetings, *demoiselles*," he said. "I already know

who you are . . . the charming daughters of the bewitching Marty and the redoubtable Philip.''

The girls, not used to such Gallic courtesy, were surprised into silence. Susannah said, ''Their names are Dorothy and Roberta. Girls, this is my distant cousin, Louis Rossignol, from Tahiti, Françoise's brother. He spent a holiday here fifteen years ago. He is also, of course, related to the Rossignols at Akaroa.'' She turned to Louis. ''The girls had a holiday there a couple of years ago with the rest of the family, staying at one of these motels Margot and Pierre Laveroux run, in conjunction with Rossignol House. It's partly a museum, and Tante Elise is still alive. I don't think you met Pierre, but you will remember tante, of course.''

''Of course. How could one forget her? But how old is she?''

Clothilde chuckled. ''Same as me. In her eighties and, like me, very well looked after. If you can stay long enough, Louis, we'll take a trip there some day. We could stay a night. We can't spare much more than that, with so much still to be done for the reunion.''

''I'm a bit hazy on things after fifteen years, but no doubt Shanna will jog my memory. If I'm to stay here I hope I won't be treated like a guest, but will be permitted to do what I can in the matter of preparing food for the great day, waiting upon guests and so on, so I can redeem my too-long neglect of my family connections. It won't be too much for everyone if I stay on, I hope?''

Clothilde said very softly, ''You are welcome for your own sake, Louis, for the little boy we loved so dearly fifteen years ago, and also for your sister's. How we all loved her! It was a terrible blow when she died and her little daughter with her. It still gives me a sense of great loss. She was so often over here and despite the difference in our age, we were such friends.''

The girls had run out to shut the ducks up for the night, so they could speak more freely. Best to get it over and done with. So much sorrow lay in the past for Louis

Rossignol. He was now the only member of that once closely-knit family of four.

He said, with some hesitation, "Is my brother-in-law still around here? I suppose I'll have to meet him?"

Morgan nodded. "He's home at present, but fortunately he's away a lot because he's taken up political interests. We see him from time to time, of course, but naturally he's not exactly our favourite person."

Susannah looked swiftly at him. He had compressed his lips. She looked at Louis. He was wearing much the same expression. But all he said was, "I hardly remember him at all. You I would have recognised immediately, Morgan."

Susannah said, "Well, of course, he was away at boarding school most of the time you were here and he was just old enough to consider us beneath his dignity. He was much nearer our age than Morgan, but where Morgan didn't mind romping with us, John did. He's a bit lonely, I think. In fact, I'm of the opinion political life in the capital would be better for him than farming. Morgan tells me the farm's not doing too well."

She was somehow trying to make excuses for John. Louis had shown a real reluctance to meet him. It wasn't fair to John. But perhaps a girl's family, given these circumstances, might feel that had she never married this man, she might still be alive. But that was unjust. Although it was rare, women did die in childbirth nowadays, and wasn't it toughest of all on the husband?

She stood up. "I'll show you to your room, Louis, then I'll put the finishing touches to the dinner. After the meal we'll take you around the garden. The nights are just beginning to give us a longer twilight."

With Louis's coming the tension slackened. Susannah and Morgan had no long hours alone. Susannah felt more natural, not always on guard lest she betray herself. It was fun too, because Louis seemed to have forgotten almost all he knew about riding, and had to be taught all over again. But he was a sport and stuck at it, and gradually the veneer of the suave businessman from Los Angeles and Tahiti peeled off, and he became less formal.

Oddly enough, Susannah wouldn't have imagined life would have taken the younger Louis that way. But perhaps she was just remembering what a daredevil he had been. Hearing from time to time of his climbing and exploring exploits, she had thought he would be a more rugged type. But he was evidently adaptable, and when his accident had frustrated his liking for forays into jungle and swamp and up great heights, he must have found more of his father in him than he'd guessed. Now he was enjoying pitting his wits against opponents in the competitive world of big business rather than against the forces of nature.

They got over the awkwardness of his meeting with John by having quite a number assemble to meet him at the homestead—all families who'd known the boy Louis. They were so glad to see once again the young French boy they'd liked so well fifteen years ago, and laughed at him because he found it hard to single them out and demanded forbearance from them and an end to the guessing games. "My old playmates have grown so handsome or so beautiful; it is not my fault. If I recognise some of you and fail to know others, then I will indeed blot my copybook, as you say. I shall pretend my head injury was more lastingly harmful than it is . . . come now, my little cousin forty-times-removed, and tell me everyone's name in turn, pointing rudely with your finger."

He said easily, when she came to John, "I could be forgiven had I not recognised you, John, because we saw very little of each other because you were in Christchurch most of the time. I hear you are interested in politics these days. What a splendid thing! Me, now, I would not do for the arena of legislation and debate, because my wits are not quick enough, but I so admire politicians, who give their services, and are often not thanked for it."

Shanna was grateful to Louis. No enmity had been noticeable. She was conscious more and more of feeling extremely sorry for John. In a community in which he had lived all his life, and his forebears before him, there seemed something lacking in almost everyone's manner towards him. She'd even heard someone say once, talking to a Linden Peaks resident about him, "He's not a Forester. He's more like his mother. Although we all tried so hard, she was never quite one of us." It had the effect of making Shanna's manner towards him warmer.

She thought John watched her and Louis rather closely from that first friendly gathering on. One day she left Louis riding with Morgan and Dan up to their pet irrigation scheme, which afforded them great pleasure. In fact they were like boys with an electric train.

Edith Raymond, John's housekeeper, had rung up to say she'd a fairly empty deep-freeze at the moment and if Shanna wanted to bring over the batches of cookies and cakes she'd been making for the big day it would leave the freezer at Larchwood with plenty of room for the other stuff—the hams and cold turkeys and corned legs of mutton the community was preparing.

Shanna quickly filled cartons with the frozen goodies and departed in the Hunter. She and Mrs. Raymond stowed the stuff, then had afternoon tea together. She was a comfortable body, with a husband whose health had forced him to retire from his own small farm, but was well able to potter around the homestead garden and oversee the young farm cadet during John's absences. They had their own quarters and John was very fortunate.

She said to Shanna, "Oh, I daresay some time we'll take a cottage in Linden Peaks, and meanwhile it keeps my man feeling he's not yet on the shelf. John can't afford a full-time manager."

Susannah nodded. "It was a great tragedy my cousin died when she did, so young. Things could have been so different. She was so lovely, Mrs. Raymond, so full of the joy of life, and it must have been a big break to leave Tahiti, and her father and brother, to settle here in such different surroundings. She wasn't a bit like Louis to look at. He took after their mother, it was said, and Françoise was like Marty Griffiths, with red hair and blue eyes and the sort of vitality that goes with that colouring. The days were full of laughter when she came here that year.''

Mrs. Raymond looked at her curiously. "I've heard that said before. But she wasn't like that when I met her. Oh, yes, I did know her. When my Douglas had to give up the farm, he was pretty sick at first, so we had a cottage at Linden for a few months. Then I was asked to come here to assist when she was expecting the baby. She was sweet, but never gay. But how she wanted that baby!

" 'It will be my very own,' she would say as she added to the layette day by day, sewing and knitting for dear life. 'It must be wonderful to be a mother, to bring a life into the world and for that child to love you in the closest of all bonds.' And she said a strange thing, then. It worried me. Not that I've ever spoken of it to anyone else. She said, 'To love you without rhyme or reason . . . not for what you have, or had, but for yourself alone.' ''

Susannah felt her brows draw together. That had been a strange thing to say. Mrs. Raymond said, "But there . . . one has all sorts of weird fancies when carrying a child.''

Susannah nodded. "So I've heard. Mrs. Raymond, I've never asked anyone else this. Everyone was so grieved, I couldn't. But you've said how Fran looked forward to motherhood. Did she know her baby wouldn't live? I've wondered if that might have taken from her the will to live, and now you've told me this, I wonder still more.''

"No, my dear, she didn't know. That much was spared her. It so happened John was in Invercargill when she took her pains. Douglas sent a message to him. He was at a meeting and couldn't be reached directly by phone.

Anyway, we weren't worried, because first babies don't usually come quickly. But this one did. We stayed on at the nursing-home. Invercargill airport was closed by fog. John left by car.

"It seems incredible now how overjoyed we were that it was over so quickly for Fran. They allowed me in to see her, as her husband couldn't be there. I've always been glad I did see her, because she looked better than she had for months, just like a picture of the Madonna I have on my bedroom wall, all ethereal and shining. They had just shown her her little daughter.

"She said, 'Edie, she's so exquisite. Not all red and wrinkled and cross as some new babies are, but just pink and white, like apple-blossom. So new and untouched . . . and mine. I'm drowsy now. How wonderful to go to sleep knowing that when I wake my little Justine will be with me—a new dimension in my life. 'Bye for now, Edie.' "

Edie Raymond wiped away a tear. "Neither of them ever woke. It was my only comfort. She had become so dear to me. I felt that she had truly found that new dimension and she'd never shed a tear over her child, as all mothers do, through the years. And I could remember always that her last conscious moments were of sheer happiness."

Shanna knew the rest of it, of course. Clothilde had written to her of the poignancy of John's arrival at the nursing-home to find both wife and daughter gone from him.

When Shanna had wiped her own tears away, she said, "Thank you for telling me this, Edie. I was never told."

"It wasn't common knowledge. Somehow I didn't want the—oh, what is the word I want? Didn't want the intimacy of those moments repeated from one person to the next . . . you know how an item like that gets bandied about . . . I did write to her brother when I heard he was out of hospital following that climbing accident. I had a

wonderful letter from him. The only others I told were
Clothilde, and Morgan Hervington-Blair."

Susannah was startled. "Morgan, Edie? Why
Morgan?"

"Because of how he felt. You know how Morgan is.
He's so compassionate. It's on account of his being a vet,
I think, Shanna. He's never become hard-boiled about
animals in pain. You'll have seen him time and again,
soothing and talking to them, like a woman with a sick
child. In those last few months it seemed to me he was the
only one who made Fran laugh. Laugh properly, I mean,
not just polite laughter."

"So Morgan knew, and Clothilde . . . and John, of
course?"

It wasn't really a question. But Edie Raymond shook
her head. "No, I told him she had said how beautiful her
baby was, and how pleased John would be with his
daughter. Any man ought to think his wife's last thought
was for him." Now she looked startled herself. "I've
never told anyone I lied about that, lass. And I hardly
know why I've told you now, except that. . . ." She
changed her mind, and said, "You'll keep it entirely to
yourself won't you?"

Shanna reached out for Edie's work-worn hand.
"Edie, I'm very good at keeping secrets. It's on account
of my father's work. Even in trade commission circles,
one hears things that mustn't leak out, or the economy
could be threatened. You paid me a great compliment by
telling me this. I loved my cousin so dearly in those few
weeks we lived together at the Vale. Edie, why did you
tell me?"

She hesitated. "I heard you once nearly married John.
I wouldn't like to think you were so . . . so sorry for him
that you . . . er . . . took him on again. Probably you're a
little tougher than Fran, mightn't bruise so easily,
but . . . well, I don't think John Forester would ever
satisfy the likes of you. I think he'll remarry, but not
anyone like Fran. He'll marry someone in the political

world, someone who'll advance his career . . . he'll weigh everything up. Who'll. . . ." She broke off, because voices could be heard nearing the house. John and Douglas and the cadet, wanting some tea.

The whole scene was unreal to Shanna . . . John looked every inch a typical farmer, kindly, uncomplicated . . . that whole poignant story couldn't pertain to this setting, surely? Fran ought to have been sitting here, handing out scones and fruitcake. Justine should have been a mischievous two-year-old, starting to talk. What had gone wrong with them all?

She herself should have been Morgan's wife, with him still at his clinic, with a home at Linden Peaks township, coming and going to her grandmother as she needed her. Only Morgan hadn't uttered the words that would have kept her here, that would have turned a sham into a lasting marriage . . . and who was she to blame Morgan? It had simply been ill-starred for them all.

CHAPTER SEVEN

Pleasant days followed, and the only ripple of uneasiness on the tranquility of Shanna's mind was what Edie had said about John and the probability that he would marry to further his political career. Had Edie been warning her that John might look her way again because, as her father's daughter, she knew so well the world of overseas trade and finance? She had a feeling this was true. She knew a distaste for herself, that she had ever been so lacking in discrimination that she had been so drawn to him five years ago. Then another doubt struck. Was she any more discriminating now?

If she was sensible she wouldn't still know these longings for Morgan. But even when they said barbed things to each other, she could still feel a wave of love, quite irresistible, sweep over her . . .

Such small things could stir it . . . Morgan sitting in the corner of the room in the evening, making fishing flies for the season shortly to open, tying them with infinite care; Morgan entering, meticulously, farm details in the journal he kept; Morgan standing by the sheep-pens, the sun on his hair, the light showing up

even the bleached hairs on his tanned and muscular
forearms ... the stocky yet easy grace of him as he
swung into the saddle, his change from rough and dusty
shepherd of the day to the debonair man of the evening,
a tribute to Clothilde who still liked their leisure hours to
smack of gracious living.

She'd gone to give him a message from one of the
stock agents one day. She knew he couldn't be far away
because she could see Lady Grey tethered to a fence-post
just where the slopes of Cabbage-tree Hill rose from the
home paddock.

There was a copse of oaks just above there and as she
neared she could see Morgan standing perfectly still at
the edge of it, calling softly in the way she'd often seen
him use for frightened animals. What was he calling to?
Not his dog, because Bluey had been asleep in his dog-
motel as she passed, just raising his head to look at her,
and lapsing again.

Susannah became motionless too. Presently, to her
amazement, a ewe emerged and came slowly towards
him, stopping in suspicion every few steps, ready to take
flight at a movement. As she neared Morgan, Susannah
had a side-view of the animal and saw she had a few feet
of barbed wire wound right around her.

Finally, the ewe came right up to Morgan. He bent
down, grasped her firmly by the wool, began unwinding
it, talking to her, meanwhile. Before he let her go he
examined her mouth, in the way of all shepherds, then let
her go, watching her bound through the trees on to the
sunlit pasture beyond.

Susannah called out, "Bravo!" and clapped her hands.
Morgan swung around and beheld her. He grinned with
a hint of boyish pleasure as if glad someone had seen him
accomplish something so unusual. He could have ridden
back for a dog, of course, to cut the sheep out for him, but
this had saved it much distress. Susannah ran up to him,
all light and glow, and held out her hands to him.

"Oh, Morgan, I was fascinated! Congratulations!"

And before she knew it, had raised herself on tiptoe and kissed him lightly on the mouth.

He laughed, still holding her hands. "I've done it before, but never with an audience. It's fatal to have anyone within half a mile. You must have frozen."

"I did. Just in time. I was terrified Lady Grey might see me and whinny."

"Good job it wasn't Louis."

She nodded. "He'd have spoiled it, without meaning to. Of course you can hardly expect him to have much savvy with the sheep, but he was so good at it when he was a kid, wasn't he?"

"So you noticed it too? As a boy he took to it like a duck to water. I used to think it was inborn, that knack, because the Rossignols, all that time ago, in Normandy, were pastoral people. But although he's riding well now, he's a real duffer with the stock. I don't think he likes the dust and dirt of yarding, to say nothing of the smells. But he's good fun, and you can't help liking him." He cocked an eye at her. "So don't fall for him, Susannah Carew. He wouldn't do for here."

She said a little coldly, "I suppose you're joking. He's a relation."

"It's distant enough not to matter, but he's a fascinating chap, so watch it. You were vulnerable once before and used less than good judgment when you fell for John. Don't let history repeat itself. These reunions engender all sorts of unreliable relationships. Louis is likeable but a lightweight, hasn't fulfilled his early potential. He'd never satisfy you. You and he have nothing in common, really."

Susannah looked exasperated. She tossed back the thick honey-coloured hair and lifted her chin in defiance. The sun shone directly in her eyes. She turned away from it a little to look sternly at Morgan.

"Oh, you and your classifications, Morgan! You draft people the way you draft sheep. You set far too much store on kindred tastes and suitability and . . . and everything. It almost seems out of character. You ought to be a nice uncomplicated son of the soil, taking pleasure in ... in primitive things ... not delving into such realms. You sound like a psychologist.''

Mischief lit his brown eyes. The little creases at each side of his mouth deepened. "And who made *you* such a judge of my character? You know something of me, but not everything, by a long chalk. How do you know I don't take pleasure in primitive urges like this, for instance ... ?''

He tugged her close, bent his head, set his mouth on hers. His hands were warm against her shoulder blades through her thin silk checked shirt. He held her so close she was afraid he would hear the pounding of her heart. He had her too fast to struggle. Suddenly she was aware that her heart wasn't the only one pounding. When he had to desist for breath, he laughed, his face just two inches from hers.

She said, "Morgan!" in a tone that was meant to sound shocked. He burst into a great laugh.

"Don't pretend you didn't enjoy that too, Susannah Carew ... come on, own up ... it was quite a kiss, wasn't it? Heavens, girl, you talk about me being too analytical, yet you equate everything I say about kindred tastes and bringing reason to bear upon marriage as adding up to only certain things ... both liking the life here, both liking poetry, both reading the same books ... you'd find we'd both like other things too. You don't know a darned thing about me, really. Now don't start arguing with me. Your applause earlier has gone to my head. Come on back and make me some afternoon tea. Making love, I find, sharpens the appetite!''

She said scornfully, "Making love! That wasn't making love ... snatching a kiss.''

"I know, but it was a good preliminary ... given other circumstances ... privacy for instance, instead of within range of those binoculars Clothilde is so addicted to, that could have led up to something more satisfying, more prolonged . . . if only I'd known I'd have called that sheep to me inside the copse . . . "

He took a look at her face as they walked down the slope, and laughed again. "You're *trying* to look outraged. You think you ought to feel that way. And you don't. You enjoyed that, didn't you? Of course you did."

She turned on him, with temper, "Why do I need to answer, when you answer your own questions? You said of course I did . . . so I won't answer you."

"You don't need to, lady fair. Silence gives assent."

Susannah choked, glared at him, attempted to say something, caught his quizzical look, and it was too much for her. She burst into reluctant laughter. He laughed with her. They stood there, helpless with mirth for a few moments.

She swayed so much, he caught her arm to steady her, then he said, quite seriously, "That's better, isn't it, girl? Nothing like laughter to sweep away all feelings of stupid and unaccountable hostility, eh?"

She nodded, wiping away tears of laughter. "Y-yes. We've been taking each other too seriously ever since I came home. I think it must have been because it was an awkward situation. Because we were once engaged. *We* knew there was nothing in it, but other people didn't and they watch us and wonder and it makes us unnatural."

Morgan nodded. "Nevertheless, I think we could begin again. Now please, Susannah, don't cut me off, or bridle again. How about a clean slate? Everything we say to each other seems coloured by the fact we had that mock relationship five years ago. It was so sudden. I pitchforked you into that. One moment you were in love with John, next you saw him looking warmly at Françoise, next you were—in the eyes of all—engaged to me. Most engagements take place after a certain period of courtship. Oh, look behind you, but not suddenly. That's what I mean . . . look at that bantam rooster, he's courting . . . he's trailing his wing in front of his lady-love . . . "

Keep still, he'd said. What a hope! Susannah
collapsed. "Oh, Morgan, Morgan, you priceless idiot!
I've had men make romantic approaches, but none of
them," her silver-clear laughter rose on the air,
" . . . none of them ever talked about *bantams* in the
middle of it!"

"Shut up!" he said. "But take note of this. *Everything*
that has happened between us till now is wiped. This
blasted reunion is going to occupy our days to the
exclusion of all else, unfortunately, which doesn't give
one much time for trailing one's wing. But through it all,
just keep remembering that's exactly what I'm doing.
You're here to stay and I'm here to stay . . . under
contract . . . and if that doesn't add up to something, it
should."

He seized her hand, began to run with her. "Now,
come and make me that tea, and don't get all uptight
with me. It's a clean slate, remember!"

She was still laughing when they ran into the kitchen
where old Clothilde was sitting with her patchwork. Her
eyes approved their relaxed air, their linked hands.

That night John rang. He was just back from Christchurch. "Shanna, would you act as hostess for me
tomorrow night? You recall the Billinghams? We met
them at that affair in Wellington. They were at this
meeting in the city, and he's addressing another in
Timaru tomorrow, and I suggested they have dinner
with me tomorrow night. Would you? This man is very
important to me."

She wished he'd not added that. She said, "Are they
staying the night with you?"

"No, they're going on to Ashburton from here.
They've a married daughter there. Will you, Shanna?
You know so well how to do these things and the
Billinghams were very interested in you because of your
father."

It would be churlish to refuse. Shanna said, "All right,

John, I'll do that for you. What time? Oh, then I'll come over half an hour beforehand. No, not earlier. I won't do the flowers and the table. Edie is so good at that sort of thing, and I wouldn't hurt her for the world. If you're going into the political arena, I think you should begin practising diplomacy, and it starts by understanding people."

John said, "This is where I need you, Shanna. I'd blunder and make a fool of myself otherwise. Bear that in mind."

She purposely misunderstood him. "Bear what in mind?"

"That I need you."

She was slightly frosty. "How nice to be needed. It's supposed to be good for one's morale." They talked on for a moment or two, then she hung up, turned from the hall phone to see Morgan on the bottom stair, looking at her.

He said, "Well, I'm glad to see you've not donned rose-coloured spectacles again. That's the difference between twenty-two and twenty-seven, isn't it, Susannah?"

How strange that this didn't ruffle her. Perhaps it was his tone—not derisive as was his wont when he spoke of John, but just glad she was taking it this way. She shrugged, "What a bore. I'm to act as hostess for him to some people we met in Wellington." She pulled a face. "I've had so much of this sort of thing. It's not my life, though I put up with it for mother and father's sake.

He came across to her. "Was that right, Susannah? Was that all it meant to you?"

"Yes."

"Then why stay on? You could have made your home here."

She smiled a little wistfully. "There's a very close bond between my parents and me. Mother followed her man, forsaking all others. She's always been nostalgic about the rivers and the plains of her girlhood. Her one dread was that she might also lose me, that I might want to stay here when I got into my teens, and that we might drift apart.

"I was their only child, Morgan. I didn't want mother to feel she'd sacrificed family too, to dad's career. In a year or two they'll be back in New Zealand for good. Dad thinks he'll get a post in Christchurch, a sort of semi-retired one, and they'll spend many weekends here. In fact they think they might build a weekend cottage on the estate. Of course we all had the idea that it could be, at grand-mère's age, she wouldn't be here to enjoy having us. At times it made us all panicky, Morgan."

Morgan said, "I think this is the time I should ask your forgiveness for thinking you were selfish for staying away so long. It's so easy to misjudge other people. I'm sorry, Susannah Rose. Don't hold it against me. I was so anxious for Clothilde."

She thought wistfully it would have been wonderful to have him add: "And I so longed to have you back here myself." But that didn't seem to be Morgan Blair's way. But she was glad he'd asked her to forgive him.

She said impulsively, looking up at him as he stood on the stair, "I can understand your thinking that. And some time when we're away out by ourselves I'll tell you more about our reasons—when grand-mère isn't within hearing—she just might come out now. And seeing you've said sorry, I should too. After all, I thought you—" she came to a sudden halt.

He looked at her curiously, saw the pink come up in her cheeks. "You intrigue me, Susannah. Don't you dare stop. You thought I what?"

The browny-green eyes looked up into his. He saw the lips part in a smile over the slightly irregular teeth . . . for a moment he saw the twelve-year-old Shanna confessing the mischief she'd been up to. He said so. She laughed. "You could be very angry with me."

He caught her hand. Contact like that always made understanding easier. "Try me," he said.

The colour deepened. "I misjudged you. I thought you were . . . oh, how shall I put it? . . . hanging after Marty while her husband was away. I was sure of it when I was coming back from Wellington with John. We saw you pulling away from the White House with her. You didn't see us. John took me on to Mata Flat, so I had quite some time to think about it. I did you a great injustice. Sorry, Morgan, you were just rushing her to join Philip."

He laughed, rubbing his thumb over the back of her hand. How strange the sense of touch was, so much less clumsy than words. At times she and Morgan had bruised each other with what they said. But in that tiny caress was some sort of bond.

He grinned, "I ought to go all self-righteous and say in stiff-necked pride that I'm not the sort to dangle after another man's wife, but I don't feel prickly about it at all. Perhaps because there was nothing in it. You stupid thing! Marty was just one of several girls I took out a few times, more as friends than anything else. I admit with Marty it could have deepened into something, but she was so straightforward—told me she wasn't interested. For instance, I took out a cousin of the Beechingtons' at Tawhai a few times, and a girl who helped the Logies at Alpenlinden after Marty got married. Can't think of her name at the moment . . . Jenny someone, I think. Or it could have been Jean. I guarantee you've been out with plenty of men in your time, especially in the sort of life you've lived . . . in more formal circles where you'd need an escort. Haven't you?"

She laughed. "Of course."

"And sometimes got kissed goodnight . . . of course again! You might even have felt your pulses flutter for some of them . . . we're geared that way. Well, that's how it was with me with Marty. I think I kissd her twice. Now, is that all you've had against me . . . of late?"

"Yes . . . at least . . . "

"Right, let's have it. Look, this is a bit less than private. Come into the farm office." He opened a door behind him, they went in. Susannah sat on the desk, swinging her legs. She had on a brown silk top patterned in green, cream crêpe trousers with a row of tucks at the full cuffs and green sandals on bare feet. She curled up her toes and regarded them thoughtfully.

He said, "Susannah, stop looking about twelve and come to the point. What else did you have against me?"

She looked up appealingly. "Morgan, promise you won't be cross with me?"

He grinned. "I'll do no such thing. I'll probably be very cross with you, but it won't last." He moved against the desk, so close she could feel the warmth of his thigh against hers. "I could be just amused, however. So go on. I like this Susannah much better than the Shanna who came home, brittle and sarcastic and very self-sufficient."

She said, "Watch it, Morgan Llewellyn Hervington-Blair! I might be the one to get cross if you go on like that. Don't try your luck too far."

"Come on, lass, give me a broadside for whatever I did wrong." He put a hand on her knee and rubbed it affectionately.

Her eyes looked into his frankly, "I didn't like your saying Françoise was so unhappy. I thought you were warning me about John . . . putting a spoke in his wheel, and unfairly at that. No, don't say anything yet, Morgan, hear me out. I know now you weren't unfair. But that first morning I was talking of Fran to John . . . oh, I didn't say you'd said anything. It cropped up because . . . well, that's rather private . . . but I asked him if Fran had been unhappy because she thought she was second choice."

Morgan looked shrewd. "Let's get this straight. I must know, so I must interrupt. I can think of only one reason for you to ask John that . . . because he told you that you'd always come first with him. A lead-up, in fact, to asking you to marry him."

"You're altogether too astute. I didn't let him get that far because I interrupted by saying I couldn't bear it if Fran had been less than ideally happy because of me. He said that if anyone had hinted Fran wasn't happy, it was only because she was so homesick for Tahiti, which sounded extremely natural. I was furious with you, because homesickness is a dreadful thing to fight. I *know*—I had to spend so long away from my very own place. I thought you'd used that misery of Fran's to try to stop me feeling so sorry for John that I once again—I'm quoting you, Morgan—let my heart overrule my judgment. But now...." she looked past him and against her will, her eyes filled with tears.

He squeezed her knee, put his other arm about her, said, "Now you know she *was* unhappy. I wish it had been otherwise. It was something we onlookers had to live with, because there was nothing we could do, except give her affection, all of us." Then he added, "But how did you find out?"

"Edie Raymond told me. It came spontaneously. You mustn't think I was prying." In her earnestness Susannah caught hold of his hand. "Edie told me that she'd told you and grand-mère and no one else what Fran said to her at the end, in that happy first ... and last ... hour of motherhood. It was a tribute to you, Morgan, that she told you. It made me realize what it must have been like, watching all that light and gaiety go out of Fran's make-up. No wonder you felt hard against me for not being here. What made Fran so unhappy, Morgan? Does the blame lie at John's door? It would be terrible to do him an injustice."

He shook his head. "I find no pleasure in telling you this, Susannah. Naturally you'll think it was sour grapes with me. You remember Louis saying his father's business had a spectacular crash? That he had such integrity that he paid back every debt, some incurred more by his partner than by himself?" She nodded. Morgan continued, "John absolutely despised him for this quixotic behaviour—he actually wrote to his father-in-law saying that by satisfying his own conscience he was depriving his son and daughter of the inheritance

they should have. He had been an extremely wealthy
man. He had paid Fran an allowance, a very bountiful
one. He wrote, with confidence in her, that of course it
would have to stop. Fran wrote back saying she didn't
need it. She actually sent him every penny she had in her
own savings account—said she had a home and a
husband now and it must all be returned to him. John
was away at the time. When he came back he cut up
rough about it, and, which was worse, wrote to the father
along those lines. He never stopped niggling about it.
When Fran found out—from her father—she was beside
herself. She just couldn't believe her husband could be so
cruel, so mercenary, so hard.

"She walked out into the night, one of those balmy
nights that up here are often the lull before an electrical
storm. She hadn't been here long enough to read the
signs, and besides, she was blind with pain. Finally John,
too tardily, organised a search. He simply said she was
fond of solitary night walks. I was the one to find her.
Fortunately, Doctor Mac was with one of the groups not
far away, but before he got to us, she gasped it all out to
me, otherwise she'd have bottled it up and perhaps never
recovered. She had double pneumonia, made a fair
recovery, but something had gone out of her.

He paused. "Susannah, I'm sorry to burden you with
all this ... I've never been one for retelling sad events for
telling's sake, but for your own sake you must know. I
wouldn't like another girl of the same calibre as Fran
used by John."

Susannah knew an anguish of her own. If only he'd
said, "I couldn't bear to see *you* used like that." But he
kept it impersonal. She shut her mind to that, suddenly
ashamed that she could think of herself at that moment,
then said, "Then that's what Fran meant. Edie mightn't
have told you this—about the way Fran looked forward
to motherhood. 'A child to love you without rhyme or
reason ... not for what you have, or had, but for yourself
alone.' "

Morgan drew her head against him. "That would be it, Susannah. But it's all over now. We mustn't grieve any more. She did know that hour she longed for. *Mignonne*, dry your eyes, we aren't meant to sorrow too long for old, unhappy, far-off things. Here's my handkerchief."

How comfortingly adequate a man's handkerchief was! She looked up. "You seem to have picked up a little of the French expressions from my grandmother. You called me *mignonne*. Oh, what's that? Morgan, it sounds like someone in the drawing-room. But who. . . ."

Morgan cocked his head to one side. Normally they'd have put the noises down to Clothilde or Louis and called out, but these noises seemed furtive, stealthy. . . .

Morgan put his mouth to her ear, whispered, "An intruder, I think. Don't move."

Very quietly for so large a man, he moved the short distance to the door into the hall, and along to the drawing-room door. Susannah, disobeying, moved silently in his wake. Morgan turned the knob very slowly, and flung it open, then both he and Susannah gasped out, "Louis!"

Louis swung around, and almost dropped the Sèvres vase he was holding, uttering a startled sound as he did so. "What on earth—" he began, but he was drowned out as both Morgan and Susannah burst out laughing.

Louis said, "Me, I do not find this funny. I could have smashed this to atoms!"

Morgan said, "Sorry, old chap, but it was with the very best intentions. We must have been seeing too many crime stories on T.V. We thought we'd caught an intruder. We were in the office, the sounds seemed so muffled, so stealthy, and our imaginations ran away with us. We were trying to protect the family treasures and almost accounted for the demolition of one of them. And, Susannah, I told you to stay where you were!"

"You dope, I couldn't have let you go in alone!"

Morgan guffawed. "Mighty midget! A game-hearted bantam cock standing up to an eagle!"

"Wrong sex," said Susannah. "You've got bantams on the brain just now. They seem to crop up at all sorts of dramatic moments."

The sherry-brown eyes glinted. "Oh, you remember that, do you? Good."

She looked away, swiftly. Louis had a frown between his brows, and no wonder. They'd gone off on a tangent. She said, "Louis, do forgive us, taking you for a burglar."

He laughed. "Idiots, I shall call you. The sounds were muffled, yes. Stealthy, no. It was just that I was, *naturellement*, picking things up and putting them down very gently, and you come bursting in like great bulls. I'm getting my sexes mixed too! Tante was telling me about some of these today, the French things she brought with her. We were trying to work out which had come here with the first French settlers and which had been brought back to Akaroa, through the years, by the descendants who had visited France."

Susannah nodded. "Some I can identify. This, for instance. I was with mother in France when she bought it to send to grand-père for his birthday, to keep his cuff-links in. But it's really a patch-box, eighteenth century, and that candlestick was given to me by one of the Rossignols in Normandy when I stayed with them."

Louis said, "Of course I am more interested in the Rossignol ones, being connected with Victorine rather than with Clothilde, who is a connection by marriage only. That vinaigrette, I imagine, is from the Rossignol side. There was one almost its twin, at home in Tahiti."

"Was?" said Susannah.

Louis nodded. "All sold to pay the debts of honour."

For a moment no one spoke. That sort of sacrifice got one with tightened throat. All the prized family heirlooms gone; yet perhaps Louis's and Françoise's father had died with a clear conscience because of that sacrifice.

Bridging that awkward moment Morgan said, presently, "Talking of the Rossignols, we must get you across to Akaroa soon. Madame rang up again today. We can treat ourselves to a couple of days off before the reunion gets too close. It will do us all good, and besides, if anything to do with business calls you unexpectedly to Auckland or Papeete, you will have seen her."

Louis said quickly, "Are you sure, *mon ami*, that you can spare the time? You say Tante Elise will be here for the big day. Would not that be enough? I was just a youngster before, and my impressions of my last visit there are so vague. . . ."

"Oh, it's no trouble. It would disappoint madame so greatly not to have you visit Rossignol House now that it's a museum, and recollections will come flooding back, I'm sure."

Susannah put in, "And you loved it so much, Louis, fifteen years ago. Even then you were interested in climbing. They left us there a few days, remember, and you took me all over Mount Bossu . . . the kindly hunchback that brings up his shoulders to protect the Bay from the Antarctic winds and so makes it possible to grow grapes and semi-tropical flowers . . . and the best walnuts in New Zealand."

"We'll make it early next week," said Morgan.

Susannah knew a great reluctance as she dressed for dinner at Forester Gorge. John would expect her to be well-dressed but not fussily. She picked out a long dress of printed Thai silk in an olive-green background patterned all over with lime-green and mimosa-gold and bark brown. Against it her pale head looked like a moth, silver-winged, in the gloaming.

Morgan said so, surprisingly, as he met her at the foot of the stairs as she came down.

She made a little face at him. "I'd much rather be a monarch butterfly, all bright orange and black. Lovely contrasts."

"Gaudy things, monarch butterflies. Beautiful in their own way, but not to my taste," said Morgan.

Susannah was swept with delicious laughter. He was so absurd, so dear, so Morgan-like. "Oh, Morgan, no one could ever accuse you of trite compliments! You wouldn't say a girl was like a rose, or a star or a beam of moonlight . . . you'd only compare her to a moth, or talk about bantam roosters."

His good-tempered mouth suddenly tightened. "You haven't any idea of what compliments I might make if I really let myself go."

Susannah felt a little pulse at the base of her throat start throbbing. She glanced up at him. "You—you seem so different from fifteen years ago, from five years ago, even."

"Of course I'm different. So are you. Fifteen years ago you were twelve to my twenty-three; five years ago twenty-two to my thirty-three, but even then we didn't—quite—meet on equal footing. I rushed you into that sham engagement, so you never saw me as anything different from the older man who'd fished you out of leaky boats and treacherous bogs and smacked your bottom, and saved you time and again from the wrath of the grown-ups who were older still . . . " his face softened noticeably, " . . . and now, I had an awful feeling I was going to have to rescue you again. I thought a couple of years had elapsed since your cousin Fran died and you were coming back to your first love. And now, even more than then, I knew him for what he was. That first time I only suspected John was on the make. I was pretty sure five years ago that he was going to give you up in favour of Fran because he'd worked it out that it would be a long, long time before you inherited Larchwood Vale, because your mother was next in line, and Françoise had a wealthy father.

"I was bitter about you for long enough, because you were staying away from your grandmother, who needed you. I thought you didn't want to come back to live close to the man you'd loved, when he was married to someone else, but I felt your concern for a lonely old lady should have made you discipline yourself to live with that. It can be done. So when you did come, when he was free, I was rough on you, very rough. But since you've been here, you've worked so hard. You're so glad to be back, so devoted to your grandmother, that against my will I was forced to the conclusion you were, after all, the woman the child Susannah had shown promise of becoming. So I'm sorry I thought those things about you. Perhaps it *would* have been too tough on you when they were first married.''

Susannah's eyes lit up. "Oh, Morgan, now I can tell you . . . I haven't had much opportunity till now. But grand-mère's listening to that radio thing, I know. She isn't to know this till mother comes to the reunion and she can see for herself that her daughter is wholly well. You see, with grand-mère losing two of her three children, we felt she mustn't know yet that she nearly lost the daughter too. Let me tell you just briefly, because time is going and seeing I promised John I'd do this, I must be there to greet his guests, but oh, how I'd rather stay home tonight. . . .''

She told him. The way his face cleared, the way his eyes lit up, she wished more than ever she wasn't due at Forester Gorge.

"That puts a very different complexion on things. It will be good when your people come and it can be told, though you were right. Clothilde would have worried terribly. I don't think she felt your continued absence as much as I did for her sake. She's so unresentful of the blows life gave her. She dwells far more on the happinesses she found. We talked of her boys one Anzac Day. I wondered if, at last, she might forgo that dawn service at the monument at the crossroads. But she went.

"I asked her then how she had borne it. She said she had accepted it as part and parcel of the times she had lived through. She said, 'Perhaps it was born in me to take such things, live through them, and not sadden others too much with prolonged grief, because after all, my forebears lived through the horrors of the French Revolution . . . and the poverty and despair of the succeeding years, till in 1840 they found a new life on the shores of Akaroa.'''

He paused and in the fading light of day she saw the flash of white teeth in his deeply tanned face. "We've got sidetracked. I was telling you we're both different now. The situation is also altered. It's more natural. We're not caught up in the falsities of a pretence relationship. You know John Forester for what he is. It's another footing altogether. But I'm not at all sure that you know *me* well. Let's take it from here, slowly."

She didn't want it slowly. She wanted to be swept off her feet, but seemingly that wasn't his way. She had to face it. It would never be a grand passion, but perhaps she was foolish to so desire it that way, to have the flame within her meet a matching flame in him, but . . . but at that instant Susannah Rose Carew knew perfectly she'd be content with less than what she desired if, some day, Morgan asked her to join her life with his.

He said now, "Blast this dinner, Susannah. Let me run you over and call for you again?"

She answered, "Morgan, I'd have no idea what time to tell you to come. I can't tell when the Billingtons will leave."

"You could ring me."

She shook her head. "That would occasion exactly what I'm trying to avoid by taking the Hunter. John wanted to call for me—that meant he'd bring me home. He'd do just that if I said I was going to ring you. No, Morgan, we've plenty of time to talk."

"Have we? Louis is always about. Oddly enough I was sure he'd want to be up and off exploring the Lake Country, even offered to ring the Beaudonais at Dragonshill to give him a weekend. I thought even if he's not climbing again yet, he'd like to see the Mount Cook region. But he didn't. Said he'd rather spend all his time here."

"That's rather nice of him. That ties in more with the Louis he used to be—very family-minded. Morgan, I must go. What a bore!"

He stood looking after her as she rushed through the hall to the Shakespeare room to bid her grandmother goodbye, and he was smiling as if his thoughts were very pleasant.

CHAPTER EIGHT

Susannah felt the evening was extremely like dozens of such dinners she'd sat through in the many cities of the world ... trade, farming, markets, tariffs, rates of exchange. Greta Billingham didn't look a bit bored. Perhaps when your own man was part of that scene, you didn't know boredom.

John was so pleased he was almost suave, a side of him new to her. Truly he'd moved a long way from his early days. For the first time she thought it wouldn't matter a scrap if Forester Gorge passed out of the hands of the family who had owned it since the eighteen-fifties.

She gave him credit for being very able; he had much knowledge at his finger-tips, and on the topics in which Bruce Billingham was most interested, he'd certainly done his homework. He would make a good politician all right, but instinct, and newly-acquired knowledge, made her realise he lacked the sincerity and integrity of a Rob Muldoon, a Keith Holyoake, a John Marshall, a Norman Kirk. But no doubt if he gained a seat, as a back-bencher he'd get cut down to size and benefit from it. She pulled herself up ... how ridiculous to make those comparisons; those men were all Prime Ministers and giants in their fields.

Later, when Edie Raymond had cleared away the remains of the excellent dinner, and they'd settled in the drawing-room, talk became more general and Susannah relaxed. Soon it became a case of the two women talking to each other while the men began going through some papers at the far end.

Greta said, "John tells me you have almost identical backgrounds, that your great-great-great-grandfathers came out on the same ship in the eighteen-fifties and travelled across the plains to the mountains, to take up this land."

Shanna nodded. "Yes, three of them. There's another estate a little further west, Blair Hills, run by the Hervington-Blairs. We have a reunion every ten years, but it's just five since the last. My grandmother's in her eighties, so it might be the last for her. Descendants of the old shipmates come from far and near."

They began talking of pioneer hazards and acccomplishments, both warming to a subject that was obviously of mutual interest. Then Greta Billingham said in a low voice, "John is a very able young man and could have quite a future in politics. But in some things he needs to make the grade. Oddly enough many up-and-coming young men are too brash and need the rough edges polished a bit. We think it's the opposite with John. He's a little too agreeable, too . . . well, for want of a better word . . . plausible." She stopped, said hesitantly, "My dear, I hope you won't be hurt by my candour. It just could be you could assist John—a woman can. He doesn't realise it, I'm sure, but it was because of this that he failed to get an overseas mission he applied for. Not a big thing, as they go, but it would have been a step up. They had a feeling that the people he'd have to contact overseas would expect men from here to be a little more rugged, more blunt. I wonder if you know what I mean? John would be *so* diplomatic he might even bend the truth a little to avoid clashes." She paused. "Oh, dear, that sounds too strong."

An imp inside Shanna made her want to laugh at this and say, "Not too strong . . . you've all unknowingly just revealed an example of this . . . he told me it was for my sake he withdrew from the chance of that post. Oh, the hypocrite!"

Instead, she said, "It's all right, Mrs. Billingham, I know what you mean. He needs to be more of a yes-or-no person."

Relieved, Greta swept on. "There may be some politicians who are born to it. Mainly though, they are made, not born. In the early days, sometimes I had to hint to Bruce there could be a better way of doing things. Mind you, with him it was usually a case of being *too* blunt. But either way, a woman can say things without the man's taking as much umbrage as he would if another member of the party suggested them. So I thought—"

Susannah knew she must break in. "Mrs. Billingham, I do hope you'll excuse my butting in, but I feel you might just go on to say something you would say only to a wife or fiancée. I am neither, to John, nor am I likely to be, ever."

Greta looked immensely surprised. "But John practically said . . . oh dear, is it only that he has ideas about you and I'm jumping the gun for him, poor dear?"

Susannah said so a little tartly and Greta was experienced enough to know the asperity was for John's presumption and not her own mistake. "Well, if *John* has ideas, I certainly haven't." She hesitated. She mustn't say anything in any way to spoil John's image. It wouldn't be fair in spite of all John had done and been. "I think I should put you in the picture. John and I were attracted to each other for a brief space of time, a few weeks only, five years ago. Quite suddenly I realised he wasn't the man for me. It was not his fault, just that we had very little in common. For my part it was wishful

thinking. My parents' life is overseas. Mine is here, at
Larchwood Vale. I thought myself into imagining I was
in love with John. Know what I mean?''

"My dear, I do. I have daughters of my own. Go on.''

"So I drew back. John eventually married a distant
cousin of mine, a French girl from Tahiti. You probably
know she died and her little daughter with her. I was my
father's secretary for years, but now he and mother are in
Canada and he's managed to get a replacement, so I
could come back to be with my grandmother. It's just two
years since Françoise died. I think John must have
thought I'd come back to ... well, console him. But I
thought I'd made it plain to him that I wasn't
interested.''

Greta nodded, her eyes full of understanding. "Pity
and sympathy aren't enough for marriage, but John
made it sound so good, your mutual background, your
experience with your father ... forgive us, we thought it
added up to much in common. But of course you've not
been back long, have you? Perhaps in time . . . .''

Susannah shook her head. "It's impossible.
I'm ... oh, how shall I put it? Well, there's someone else
in my life and there couldn't be anyone but him. I can't
say more just now.''

Greta patted her knee. "No, of course not. I take it you
are just hovering on the brink of the real thing?
Delightful days, full of enchantment and misgivings and
heights and depths. We women know. At this stage,'' she
cast a look at her husband's back, "Bruce and I look so
settled, so content, but we had our ups and down in our
courting days, too. That was what made me so certain
that what John said was fact, not wishful thinking on his
part ... because when you greeted us tonight, you had
the aura of a girl in love.''

Colour ran up into Susannah's cheeks. "That's sweet
of you. I'd hate any word of this to be hinted to John, but
in private you could perhaps tell your husband there's

nothing between John and me. Nor is there anything definite with this other attraction, yet, but . . . ."

"I know. But I wish you well, and I'll say nothing to anyone but Bruce. Nevertheless, if ever as a friend of long standing you get the chance to advise John, it could be on these lines: in New Zealand we like our politicians rugged rather than suave; sincerity and integrity count for more than the power to sway with personal charm. John has a great asset, a voice that is . . . um . . . what is the word I want? . . . mellifluous. People could fall under its spell. But it's not enough. It's *what* you say that really counts, not *how* you say it. I've known politicians with voices like corncrakes win the confidence of the people, because their innate honesty and desire to serve the people rather than to wield power and further their own ends have been evident."

Susannah looked at Greta with great respect. "Mrs. Billingham, I think your husband was fortunate in his choice of a mate. Perception such as yours must have stood him in great stead many a time. I'm not the one to say these things to John, though. But you may be able to some time and if he follows your advice, he'll be the better man for it. Oh, I think they're coming back to us."

The next hour was most harmonious. Bruce and Greta led the conversation on to those topics Susannah most understood from her long association with overseas trade. John looked at her most appreciatively from time to time. Shanna avoided his eyes. She knew exactly what he was thinking: that as a wife she'd be a great asset.

At last their guests were leaving. She was determined that as soon as they were gone, she'd be off too, so when she took Greta to the bedroom where she'd left her bag and coat, she picked up her own fleecy white jacket.

John, in the hall, looked surprised and disappointed. "I thought you might stay on a little, Shanna, seeing I haven't the privilege of seeing you home."

"I don't want to be late, John. I've people sitting up for me."

"I thought they'd have gone to bed, at your grandmother's age particularly; and Morgan's an early riser."

"Oh, he and grand-mère and Louis are real stop-ups. Don't you remember that grand-père and grand-mère were always that way? They loved their evening hours. They said they were such good sleepers, short rations did them, and if you weren't careful in farm life it was all sleep, eat, work, but the after-dinner hours of reading and discussion made up for it."

Bruce said with a glance at his wife, "We're just the same. We have so many nights out, separately, it's agreed that whoever is in first stays up for the other and we have an hour or two of companionship before bed. Odd, how after thirty years of marriage we still have so much to say to each other. Dear me, I'm rumbling on! You'll think I'm a bore."

"She won't," said Greta, "she speaks the same language. But we must go. I hate people who keep saying that and stay a quarter of an hour more. Goodnight, my dears."

John's hand, warm on her arm, stayed Susannah. He called a last goodnight, shut the door firmly. "Shanna, you're not getting away as easily as that. It's nonsense. Louis and Morgan get more than their fair share of your company as it is. I won't take no for an answer. I feel you're treating me very shabbily these days."

She said exasperatedly, "John, I'm not! I'm flat out with the preparations for the reunion. There's a big house to look after and four people to cook for. We've got to fit in two days at Akaroa before the event too; I think you ought to be grateful I came tonight, especially as, in fact, I'm so enjoying complete freedom from the world of finance and trade."

The expression on his face was almost ludicrous. "But you've known it for so long. It's part of your natural habitat. It's—"

"It's nothing of the kind. Larchwood Vale is my

natural habitat . . . a garden full of fragrance, the
mountain air, a horse beneath me, paddocks full of
white-fleeced sheep, the dust and grime of the sheep-
pens, the sheer hard work of mustering and shearing, the
sweat and heat of haymaking . . . oh, the bliss of no more
long hours at typewriters, of mingling with business
tycoons, interminable receptions and dinners and
speeches . . . it's very necessary and the breath of life to
my father, but not to Susannah Carew. My life is at the
Vale and is always going to be from now on."

"What do you mean, always? Is Morgan in this?"

"Morgan's my grandmother's manager. But I'm here
to stay. I'm hoping we'll have grand-mère for another
decade; we're a long-lived family in the main. And in a
couple of years or so my parents will be home, building a
weekend cottage on the estate. We'll be a family again."

"Will that satisfy you for long? You're twenty-seven.
Don't you want marriage, children?"

"I want marriage, children, yes. But only with the
right man. Otherwise I'd stay single all my days, as other
women have done, rather than take less than the best."

"Does it have to be less than the best?" The
mellifluous voice was at its most caressing. "Your
mother loved the Vale too, but wasn't afraid to follow her
man into political life. We could come back often enough
to stay at Larchwood Vale, especially as with your
parents home soon, your grandmother wouldn't need
you so much."

Something hit Susannah. She blinked. "John, what do
you mean? You aren't giving up Forester George, are
you?"

He fell silent, his eyes studying the carpet. Then he
looked up "Let's say that it's giving me up. Not yet. But
by the time it does, by the time certain payments fall due,
your parents could be on the way home, and I'm going to
get a post in Wellington. Actually, I've just heard. It's
being created as a part-time one, at first. Shanna,
wouldn't you come with me? If we were away from

here . . . from Morgan Blair . . . I'm confident we could attain our old idyllic state. See how brave I've been? I've not tried to lure you into resuming our old relationship by promising you that we would live here, with just periodic visits to the capital like other politicians. I've been completely honest with you."

She looked him straight in the eye then. "It's a pity you weren't as honest as that sooner. All that guff about giving up the chance of that overseas post when you heard I was coming home! You didn't get that appointment. Greta Billingham told me. She said you almost did."

John looked aghast, as well he might. "You didn't tell her I'd told you that?"

"No, it just cropped up."

He looked worried. "How did it crop up? I hope you weren't indiscreet."

She shook her head. "No, you were, when you told Greta and Bruce that we were practically engaged. She thought that, as your future wife, I might be able to let you know why you didn't get it. That I might be able to drop a hint on the qualities they think you lack." She looked at him shrewdly. "They'd prefer a man with a wife for this post in Wellington, I suppose!" She saw by his discomfiture that the shot had gone home.

She continued, "I tried to stop her, said it wasn't *my* duty to tell you; that there was nothing on my side whatsoever, nor was there likely to be. You might as well know, because it may help you, that the reason you didn't get that mission is because they feel the overseas contacts expect from us more sincerity, more rugged-ness—not suavity. John, that's what's going to be lacking in your political life if you don't take a pull on yourself. As for downright lying, telling me you'd turned it down because I was coming home—that's despicable.

"You're never blunt enough. You're afraid you'll offend people who may be useful to you, so you waver. I noticed it in Wellington. You always have on eye the

main chance. I don't like that sort of thing in people who
govern our land, make our laws. I certainly wouldn't
stand for it in a husband, I can tell you. In world politics
lately there's been too much of chicanery, fraud, double-
dealing. People from now on are going to look for
politicians who are honest, who want to run the country
for the people's sake, who are unselfish and sacrificing,
who don't love power for power's sake. It won't be
enough for you to sway people with a good voice.
There'll have to substance and integrity in what you say.

"We can't warm up those old ashes, John, and you
must stop trying. We weren't just a young couple who
quarelled. I gave you up because I realised we weren't
suited."

"You gave me up because you'd succumbed to an
infatuation for an older man."

Her voice was clear and steady. "It wasn't an
infatuation, John. It was true love on *my* part. When
Morgan and I worked on that booklet together, I found
out. But I made a mess of my relationship with him and
we parted. You might as well know, John, that for me
there's never been anyone since, nor will there be, ever.
I've never gotten over him. There, that's cleared the air.
You may find someone else, John. I hope you will.
Only please, for her sake, love her for herself alone,
not for what she has, or whether she can future your
career or not. Love her more than you love yourself,
John. It's the only possible basis for marriage . . . each
loving the other more than self. Now I'm off. Have a chat
with Greta some time. She knows her stuff. Those were
mostly her ideas I unloaded just now, even if they're
things I've known a long time. But be humble when you
ask her. Don't be on the defensive. You have gifts all
right, but play fair." And on that, she had the door open,
and was gone.

As she drove out the massive gates, she felt her spirits lift.
It was as if one chapter of the clogging past had ended

and another was about to begin. Except for that dinner engagement she and Morgan might have gone on talking . . . they might have gone outside down that moonlit path to the larch copse . . . yes, there was a full moon. Not a September moon but a November moon. Lilac and jasmine would have scented the air, the native white clematis would have glimmered out through the darkness like little stars, the pennyroyal giving up its crushed perfume as they walked . . . she would take him as she found him, and hope that some day he might come to love her as she loved him, passionately, totally committed.

As she turned up the drive towards the homestead, she saw a light in the drawing-room. Oh, surely Louis and Morgan weren't still discussing antiques! As she went over the second lot of cattle-stops, the rattly ones, the light went out and before she took the bend for the stable-yard, a light sprang up in Louis's room. Oh, good. At least he was off to bed. Despite Clothilde's love of late hours, if she hadn't retired yet she soon would. That would leave Morgan and Shanna alone.

The kitchen was empty, horribly empty. Her eye fell on a note on the table. It merely said: "Eleven p.m. Called away to Tawhai Hills. Rowena Beechington has a prize sow in trouble. Don't sit up for me—could be a long job. The others went off to bed early because we had a ring from Rossignol Bay. They want us to go there tomorrow, staying one night. So you'd better get some beauty sleep. Morgan."

For one moment she felt horribly flat, then as she took in the full import of the message, laughter had its way with her. Really, what a courtship . . . bantams trailing their wings. Pigs in trouble. Bother Rowena and her farrowing sow!

As she trailed upstairs doubts returned. Was it courtship? Oh, yes. He'd said it was. But one thing she was sure of now, though she didn't know why, was that he wasn't courting her because she was the grandaughter of the estate on which he was manager. No, it would be for herself. He still had a son's share in the Blair estate. That would have given him enough income all these years to pay a substantial deposit on a farm of his own, had he wanted that. But his regard for her grandmother kept him here.

She slipped out of her dress, hung it up, then, padding across to her dressing-table, became aware of a perfume that had nothing to do with the vase of wallflowers grand-mère had put on her bedside table.

Then she saw it. Beside her brush and comb lay a twist of lilac-coloured tissue and square in the middle of it something green and deep purple ... a sprig of penny-royal. She stood entranced. Only one person could have done that, only one to whom it could have meant anything at all. Morgan! Was it possible that that night, under that long-ago September moon, had meant more to him than she had known?

Susannah banished the wallflowers, put the penny-royal on her bedside table. She didn't want anything to overlay the sweetness of that moment. She wouldn't even read. Oh, yes, it was courtship all right.

It was a glorious morning and in spite of the four hours' sleep Morgan confessed to, he looked fit and well, and as eager as a schoolboy for the break ahead of them. "Good to go suddenly like this, otherwise you women would wear yourselves out preparing, baking stuff to take with us, doing washing and ironing ... this way we take off as fresh as new paint. We'll take a picnic lunch so we don't have to waste time on the way. Just drop that cold chicken and lettuce and tomatoes into the cooler, and some cookies and flasks, and we'll have it at Birdlings' Flat, so Clothilde can have an early glimpse of the sea ... remember how it roars up against the cliffs there? Then we'll make our way in leisurely fashion over the hill-top to Akaroa Harbour. It's too beautiful to hurry. I

always feel I go into another world when I go to Akaroa.
They ought to call it Little France."

They cut in towards the coast just past Rakaia, and had
their picnic, revelling in the tang of salt air and the surge
and abandon of that wild strip of boulder-strewn coast
stretching down south for ninety miles or more, away
from the Peninsula.

The landscape gentled as they took the road again,
with verdant valleys folded into sheep-dotted hillsides
where prosperous-looking homesteads gleamed immac-
ulate through plantations of English trees and Australian
gums. The day grew hotter, not a breath of wind to
disturb it. Clothilde's eyes were shining. She was going
back to the scenes of childhood where streets were rues
and houses with French gables clustered together. A
place where now and then even children with New
Zealand accents who spoke only English occasionally
used an expression that was unmistakably French.

From force of habit as they came to the Hilltop Hotel,
Morgan pulled into the car-park to savour the whole
panorama spread below.

Susannah said, "There isn't anywhere in the world
quite like it. I've seen so many seas, so many harbours,
but this is so truly opalescent—so many blues, so many
greens, according to the depth of the water, perhaps, or
due to its being a volcanic crater before the sea rushed in.
It still has those streaks of pure burgundy. I've never
known what causes that. Is it some trick of shadow,
Morgan, or vegetation?"

"I don't know, Susannah. I've always just accepted it.
But it certainly adds charm."

She said, "You've let me down. You've never failed
me yet." She turned to Louis. "He's a living source of
quotations for poets."

Morgan's cheeks creased with laughter. "She's doing
things for my morale. You nit, Susannah, I've only to do
a crossword to know my knowledge is abysmal."

"It isn't. Phenomenal is the word; not only is he a

voracious reader, but he has the most retentive memory
I've ever come across.''

"I envy him that," said Louis.

Clothilde was happy, happier than for five years, when
her darling *petite-fille* had left New Zealand with
shadows under her eyes and a broken engagement
behind her that should have, in time, become a marriage.
Because it was so right.

They weren't driving into Akaroa itself today. They
would turn right at Duvauchelle, a dreamy bay at the
base of a green triangle that ran back into a tree-sweet
valley. There was a cluster of buildings and houses. They
took the turn and were on the far shore of the harbour.

They drove in silence, not wanting to disturb
Clothilde's absorption in these scenes she loved so well.
There was a brimming tide, sea-birds wheeling and
swooping, clouds scattering and amassing in an azure
sky, with hills carved out against it as with a loving
finger. Across the water the sun gleamed on the pastel-
tinted houses and red and green and orange roofs of old
Akaroa.

They skirted a headland and came into Rossignol Bay.
There was Maison Rossignol built just a little back from
the sea, its wooden walls painted dazzling white, black
facings round the French windows, steep gables
intersecting a green-tiled roof, that in the long-ago had
been shingled, with shingles split from *totara* slabs.
Madame's garden almost foamed around it with a
luxuriance of leaf and bloom that love and hard work
had nurtured over the years.

The spiciness on the balmy air came from the stocks
and mignonettes and cinnamon pinks. One or two
Bourbon roses had already opened their petals to shed
their fragrance on the air; the Normandy poplars cast
long shadows on the green sward before the door.
Wisteria draped plumy boughs over garden arches,
azaleas and rhododendrons glowed from the shrubb-
eries, and on each side of the centre path of flat water-

worn beach stones were blazing beds of ground-hugging livingstone daisies, opening luxuriantly to the afternoon sun.

The door was flung wide and there they stood . . . madame very soignée and elegant still, an impression of height but conceding to age now by using a walking stick. Margot was wearing white slacks with a rose-coloured floral top over them, her golden-brown hair tied back with a gauzy pink bow, her soft brown eyes ashine. Pierre, dark, with a jutting chin, was holding a sunny-haired sprite of a child in his arms, little Elise, madame's namesake.

The greetings were most affectionate. Madame held up her face to the visitor from Tahiti. "Ah, Louis, after all these years! A score—no, fifteen, of course. But come in."

They went into the living quarters, extended now, at the rear of the museum, where they sat in a room that opened out on a patio where trees gave them utmost privacy—a huge mulberry, walnuts, oaks, chestnuts. Stone walls were covered with moss and creepers, and provided safety for the little one. Margot served them thin sandwiches with crisp cucumber and lettuce palely green between the bread, French pastries, cream kisses. Madame said, "It makes me so happy to have once again someone called Louis within this garden. I think I would have recognised you anywhere, even if the adventurous little boy of all those years ago now wears a polish and dignity unsuspected then!"

They laughed. "And after we have eaten, my dear boy, and talked ourselves out a little, we will go into the museum and you will once again see all those treasures you so loved when you were here long ago." She said to Morgan, "It was good to find in a younger generation so much appreciation of old things. Some boys would not have recognised many pieces, but Louis did. He could put a name to so many, even their periods, and could tell me which of the treasures in his father's home had their counterpart here."

Susannah happened to be looking at Morgan and saw a strange expression cross his face. What was it? Amazement, she thought. Then she clicked. Louis had been greatly interested in their pieces, but not in the least knowledgeable.

Louis laughed. "You may not think so much of me in that regard, now, Tante Elise. That crack on the head I got, which put me out of climbing, has muddled me mightily. The doctors say much of what I have forgotten will come back, but I find it so tiresome. Such stupid things I forget. Yet at the time I did not suffer from amnesia. It was only later that I became aware that in little pockets, I have no memory at all."

At that moment little Elise fell down the steps and had to be rescued. It was a golden afternoon and here, as always, they seemed to move in another world. Margot nodded and said dreamily, "Yes, because in Akaroa the past is only yesterday." She added, "That was the sentence that captured my imagination most when Pierre gave that lecture in Chelsea. And living here and looking after the wee museum, it will always be with us. We're going up to the farm for dinner. That's why dad and my stepmother aren't here. Justine is preparing the meal. She's a darling, as Irish as ever and as warm-hearted. The girls will be there too. They're looking after our motels for us, but it's a slack time. They came here straight from school today. Leonie and Sharlie are both teaching right here. Isn't it good?"

That evening Shanna realised how often Morgan had brought Clothilde here when Justine said, "You don't have to be shown your room, Morgan." But what underlined it most for her was when Tante Elise said, looking out of the window, "Dusk has now fallen. The hour I love best, when everyone who has ever lived here seems here still. Morgan, read me the poem about dusk in Akaroa. You read so beautifully. But you've said it so often to please the whim of an old lady, you must know it by heart, *hein*?"

Morgan crossed to a bookcase, removed a volume and turned to Mona Tracey's poem. "I'll try it, but I'll keep this open in case I slip up." He went to the window-seat, sat close to Susannah because there wasn't much room, put the open book on his knee but turned to look over the purpling shadows and began:

> At dusk in Akaroa town,
> When embered sunset smoulders down
> And softly wreathes the evening mist
> In whorls of tender amethyst,
> The air is charmed with old-world spell
> Of chanting bird and chiming bell;
> And garden plots are redolent
> Of poignant, unforgotten scent,
> Where gillyflower and fleur-de-lys
> Bloom underneath the cabbage-tree,
> And crimson rata tries to choke
> With amorous arms the hoary oak,
> And jonquil mocks the kowhai's gold—
> Ah, sweet it is . . . so young, so old!
>
> So young, so old! So old, so new!
> I wonder, at the fall of dew,
> When from the evening's grey cocoon
> Comes glimmering forth the moth-like moon,
> And winds, upon the brooding trees,
> Strum soft, nocturnal symphonies,
> If kindly ghosts move up and down
> In tranquil Akaroa town;
> If *voyageurs* from storied France
> Bestride the streets of old romance,
> If laughing lads and girls come yet
> To dance a happy minuet;
> If Grand-père muses still upon
> The fortunes of Napoleon,
> And Grand-mère by the walnut tree
> Sits dreaming on her rosary?

Susannah had heard the poem before, but never in Morgan's voice, so never with such enchantment. The spicy perfume of pinks and stocks, tante's "gillyflowers," came up to them.

Clothilde said, "We have much for which to be thankful, Elise. So many old people today have young folk growing up around them who have no feeling for the past, who are not kindred in any way. Oh, the young must be of their generation just as we were of ours, but we have been so fortunate that ours are so kindered."

Susannah felt a stirring at her heart. Morgan was not kin to these people of French ancestry, but it was Morgan Clothilde was referring to and there was sheer affection in Tante Elise's eyes as they rested upon him. All this was building up something within Susannah. A knowledge that love has many voices. One was the quick declaration, the urgent speech, the clamorous need that found outlet in words. That, perhaps, was the way most women wanted it, because at heart they were romantic. But another was the slow-growing, steady devotion. That was Morgan's way. He was going to offer her that, and she was going to take it.

Madame Rossignol said, "Indeed, Clothilde, we have been fortunate. The years that have taken our sons away, yours and mine, have also restored and renewed so much. Me, for instance, I thought there was no one left to carry on the name, no one to care about these things that mean so much to me, then François came . . . from another branch of the family, and he changed the anglicised form of his name back to what it should have been. And his Justine was all I could have asked for in a daughter-in-law. Then Margot . . . led to us by *le bon Dieu* . . . is it quaint to believe that these days? Well, brought here because of what some would call a chance meeting with Pierre . . . she came, and because of that, I live in this place still, with all my imperishable memories of my Louis."

Susannah was glad of the deepening shadows. She

turned her face to the window, hoping the tears wouldn't spill over. She felt surreptitiously for her handkerchief, but failed to find it. Morgan was sideways to the window too, and her back was resting against him. She found a handkerchief poked through between her waist and the windowsill. Morgan's voice said so low no one else could hear, "I like women with active tear-ducts. Can't stand the cold ones."

She turned her face completely to the window, said over her shoulder, "The harbour must be so still tonight; the lights reflected in it are perfect." She mopped at her eyes and gave the handkerchief back. Talk broke out in the other part of the room, among François's second family, Charlotte and Léonie, Jules, and Jules's fiancée, Bridget Connelly, who would bring more Irish strain into the family and please Justine.

Under cover of it Susannah said to Morgan, "I'd not realised how much a part of this scene you are, Morgan. It was good of you, these past five years, to bring my grandmother here often."

Their faces were close, so the whispering sufficed. "It wasn't entirely for her sake, Susannah, to be honest."

"What do you mean, Morgan?"

He hesitated. "This is probably not the time and the place to tell you. On the other hand, with people near you can't look disbelieving and scathing. Because you kept in touch so regularly with Justine and your Tante Elise. It gave me news of you."

The timbre of his voice had deepened. She could hardly believe her ears, but that tone was so sincere. She swallowed. "But Morgan, I wrote once a week to grand-mère, sometimes more."

"Yes, but what you wrote to Justine and madame was extra. I was so hungry for news of you."

She was silent. It seemed as if, at last, happiness was coming her way, quietly, without fireworks, but happiness. But she was still afraid of it. She had disciplined her feelings too long.

Morgan continued, "Susannah, there's an awful lot of undergrowth to be cleared away, isn't there, after that fiasco five years ago? Ever since coming home you've had to look at things in a different light. I had to give you time to look at John in a different way too. Last time I rushed things, big blundering idiot that I was. You didn't know your own mind. I'm not rushing them this time. I wish the reunion wasn't so near. I don't want to get the big decision of your life all snarled up with the organisation of that, this time. But after the reunion. . . ." Tantalisingly he stopped.

Susannah said, "Morgan, don't stop there, please."

"I'm tempted to go on, but I won't. Not in a crowded room."

She said, and her whisper was so low, he had to bend his head to catch it, "After the reunion we must talk. I think I may have things to tell you too, things that will surprise you. They can wait till then."

He moved even closer, said, "But you must tell me this now . . . are they things I'll like to hear?"

He could hear the smile in her voice as she answered him. "I hope you'll like to hear them . . . you can't turn a girl down twice!"

"What?" He raised his voice a little. She said, "Shhh!" as the sound of animated voices suddenly dropped. Then Leonie said, "Stop whispering, you two. It's bad manners. Morgan, we want you to play for a sing-song."

He grinned, rose, said, "Provided I can pick my own songs I'll do that for you, brat," and switched on the wall-light above the piano, and from memory swung into "O Susannah, don't you cry for me. . . ." He looked back audaciously at Susannah, one brow raised. He didn't know she'd ever cried for him, but now she had an idea that she'd never need to shed another tear for loneliness.

Later madame began talking to Louis about the Tahitian connections. "So many of the ones who could not settle in Tahiti but sailed on to make their home there did not keep in touch, but we were lucky, because it's a pity when links are broken. It was fascinating to meet you as a small boy and later Françoise, and especially to find her so like Marguerite Rossignol, Victorine's sister—red hair and all. So surprising to find so strong a resemblance generations later."

Louis nodded. "Yes, I was amazed myself to see that picture of Marguerite. It couldn't be more like my sister, except for the difference in dress. People rarely took us for brother and sister; Fran was so red-headed, I was so dark. But of course I took after my mother's people, the de Courcys. There is no likeness to the Rossignols in me at all."

Madame said, "I would not say there was none. I noticed it when Françoise came here five years ago. I was reminded of you by the turn of her head, and the shape of her hands, and ... " Suddenly she faltered. They put it down to the poignancy of remembering Françoise, who had not found happiness in New Zealand. She said, recovering, "I had said I would go through the treasures that are connected with the first family, Louis, but the time has gone. You and I will go through them tomorrow morning. But now the girls have made a splendid lot of confections that are as good to look at as to eat, so we must do them justice. That's something I never cease to be thankful for, that I do not suffer from indigestion."

Margot said, springing up, "And neither do you put on weight, so you are very satisfying to cook for, tante."

Susannah slept dreamlessly and deeply, even if she had lain awake for a delicious hour, recalling all Morgan had said. Perhaps he wasn't the type to be swept off his feet; witness the way he'd taken his rejection by Marty all those years ago. He'd told her how he had missed her; how he had gone over to Akaroa to glean more news of her ... oh, without a doubt something beautiful and tender was going to come to a late flowering ... spring was a lovely time, of course, sap rising, buds bursting, nature being prodigal with leaf and bloom, but in the cycle of the year Septembers gave way to summer days, full of mature blossom . . . and Clothilde had said once that she herself loved autumn best. What would have happened come autumn in April? she wondered.

CHAPTER NINE

While madame and Louis had their time among the
treasures the next morning, Pierre and Margot conducted Morgan and Susannah round the old-world
garden that surrounded Maison Rossignol and reached
back into a delightful backdrop of trees, with Puke-
o-mapu, the Hill-of-the-Sighing, rearing up to shelter it
from the rough winds of the sea. Justine was looking
after little Elise at the farmhouse, and François
Rossignol had taken Clothilde into Akaroa to have lunch
with some Lemoine relations. Morgan and Susannah
and Louis were to join them there.

Susannah, who was familiar with other French
gardens, realised afresh how traditionally French this
was indeed . . . the little walks that threaded the
shrubbery, the lavender, the rosemary, the mignonette,
the tinkling fountain and the mossy little cherub.

She said now, "What I missed most when we had to
have flats right in London was a garden. But London is
so enriched with trees, and window-boxes, it helps. I can
see now some buildings in Suffolk Place between
Trafalgar Square and the Haymarket, where we so often

walked on our way to New Zealand House, old buildings
still bearing the scars of World War Two in chipped
stone, with boxes of golden daffodils and purple grape-
hyacinths beneath them, in April.''

Madame joined them presently. She said, "Margot,
you and Pierre are wanted at the motels. One of the
helpers has found a fridge is not working as it should.
Louis has borrowed Jules's Mini and gone into Akaroa
to the museum to check up on something, so now I can
join you in my garden." They paced among the plots.

Susannah said, "Most of all I love the little crazy
paving paths that run through the shrubbery because you
brush past all the most fragrant flowers, and with sprigs
of so many in the crevices, they give off perfume as you
pass. Just like Morgan said last night . . .

> And garden plots are redolent
> Of poignant, unforgotten scent. ''

Morgan said, looking down at the paving, "One little
herb you've not got here, Elise, is pennyroyal. We have it
growing wild at Larchwood. I must bring you some."

He glanced swiftly at Susannah. She said, smiling,
"Yes, of them all I love pennyroyal most."

Elise looked from one to the other, sensing something.
Then she said, "My garden has always reminded me of a
poem in my scrapbook. I know it by heart. I must have
had it since the nineteen-thirties, those happy days
before my boys gave up their lives on the Normandy
beaches their forebears came from. But I must not speak
of sadness today. Old sorrows are like old shoes; they do
not hurt as much as when new. And I have their joyous
boyhood to remember.

"The verses were by a New Zealand poet called Cox, I
recall, and the title was *The Dream.* I wondered if it was a
true-life experience or wishful thinking. I loved it
because it embodied my own garden. I used to think that
if in old age I was shut in from my garden, I would repeat

this to myself and capture the sights and sounds of my younger days. This was my father's garden, of course, because I too was a Rossignol and married a distant cousin from France." She said, in her frail, thin voice that somehow suited the poem:

I remember that day when I walked in a garden with
    you where lavender grew;
And we dreamed a sweet dream, and we dreamed
    that the dream would come true;
      And an Idyll uprose,
      As a fair building grows,
Of a home in a garden with lavender bushes like
    those.
      So, coming and going,
      With lavender growing,
      And sea-breezes blowing,
We dreamed—till the dream fell to bits in a bolt
    from the blue.

Yet again we have come to that garden where
    lavender grew, I am walking with you,
And we dream the old dream, but the dream that we
    dreamed has come true.
      We have gained our estate.
      On this wonderful date,
For the Lord of all lovers in gardens has opened the
    gate
      For our gracious ingoing,
      With lavender growing
      And soft sea-winds blowing,
To build our home-idyll, our sweet broken Idyll
    anew.

They were silent when the beautiful voice with its faint trace of a French accent had ceased. Morgan finally broke the silence, saying, "Susannah is having trouble with her active tear-ducts again. Not to worry, *mignonne*, I told you last night I don't like hard-boiled women."

She blinked her tears away, coloured a little, said hastily, "Oh, it so fits the set-up here. The lavender growing, the soft sea-winds blowing...."

Tante Elise added softly, "And the Idyll, my dear ones, the Idyll. I think yours, like that one written of so long ago, was broken. But time has a habit of mending things, *hein*?"

Morgan said, entirely without embrassment, "It has, Elise. Our ravelled sleaves are being knitted up again. Shakespeare has it that sleep does that, but with us it seems to have been the atmosphere of that gathering last night. We haven't quite talked it out yet, my dear, because there's so much to do between now and the reunion. Last time it got snarled up about then. This time we're going to wait till all the shouting and the tumult die, and Larchwood settles down again into the usual tenor of its ways."

Elise Rossignol looked down the harbour to the infinity of ocean beyond. "You won't forget, my dears, that time is running out for Clothilde and me. Any day now we may hear that call to set our sails...." Then she added, forsaking gravity for mischief, "But when the time comes, Susannah, do remember that the cream taffeta dress in the glass case at the head of the stairs was Victorine Rose's wedding-gown ... and inch for inch, in colour and feature, you are Victorine all over again. There, it is too bad of me, I am forestalling Morgan."

Morgan's sherry-brown eyes were alight with laughter. "You're a very naughty old lady, but we shall forgive you. I'll attend to the matter when Larchwood settles into quietness again, and Louis has gone home."

Madame's face changed. "Ah, Louis!" she said, and something in her voice made them both look at her sharply. "It is about Louis that I must speak to you, Morgan. Susannah, my dear, would you mind if I spoke to Morgan alone? Only he can advise me on this. You will not take offence, *chérie?*"

Susannah laughed. "Never. I'll go on up to the farm, tante."

Morgan picked her up there. He had Tante Elise with him. Although they chatted all the way in to Akaroa, Susannah had the distinct impression that their thoughts were elsewhere. Oddly, it didn't worry her. She had other, happy thoughts to occupy her. She thought perhaps tante wanted to make a gift to Louis of one of the Rossignol heirlooms, and wanted Morgan's advice—to find out, for instance, if he thought some member of the family here would disapprove. She herself would be most happy. It seemed terrible that the Tahiti family had lost theirs to repay a debt of honour.

They saw the red Mini parked outside an antique shop. Morgan slowed, they looked in and saw Louis talking to the owner. "Didn't you say, madame, that he was going to the Langlois-Eteveneaux Museum?"

"Yes, because he thought it might be crowded this afternoon, and the lunch might drag on and he'd miss out. He can't have spent any time there."

Susannah said, "Shall we stop and let him know that Madeline Lemoine's lunch might spoil if he's late? I remember her soufflés. Pity if one should flop."

Madame shook her head. "If a soufflé is in any danger of collapse and Louis is unmannerly enough to be unpunctual, then we shall start without him. I myself mentioned Madeline's soufflés to him, and said a quarter to one, not later. I would prefer not to stop."

Susannah had a strange feeling. She had experienced it last night when they were having those delicious bedtime snacks—a feeling that Tante Elise did not like the mature Louis as much as she had certainly liked the young Louis. She had so loved him then, for himself as

well as the fact that he bore her husband's name. Come
to think of it, if Susannah was honest, she too preferred
the young Louis. There had been something so
engagingly open about him. He hadn't cared much for
money, even though his family had been wealthy. He'd
loved the simple life of the estate. But this one weighed
up everything in terms of value . . . how much was one
getting for wool these days, no not so much a bale, but
how much was that lot worth? How did the beef market
pan out? Were they badly affected by American tariffs
and quotas? Was there any way of getting around these
things, shipping the stuff to other more open markets for
re-entry as processed meat?

Neither she nor Morgan had liked it. In fact Morgan
had been very sharp with him about it. As for handling
the heirlooms at the Vale, there had hardly been a piece
Louis had admired for its intrinsic beauty, only for its
worth. Suddenly into her mind flashed the memory of
coming home from John's to see the drawing-room light
go out, then Louis's bedroom one come on, then reading
Morgan's note which said the others had gone to bed
early. It hadn't been early, though. Susannah stopped her
racing thoughts. Perhaps Louis hadn't been able to sleep,
wasn't used to early nights, and had come down for a
book to read.

Louis didn't commit the crime of unpunctuality where
soufflés were concerned. It was a magnificicent one—a
fish soufflé and the fish just caught that morning. The
sauce that went with it was every bit as good as any she'd
had in French restaurants, fragrant and tangy with
herbs, bland as cream, delicately coloured with goodness
knew what.

Louis kissed the tips of his fingers to her. "A true
Frenchwoman!" He seemed somehow a little elated.
Why? Could it have been that the antique salesman had
given him high values for antiques still in his possession?
But he'd said they were all gone. She was sure Tante Elise
and Morgan were watching him closely. She felt

uneasiness creeping over her, which deepened when Louis said, "My word, that museum was so fascinating I found it hard to tear myself away. Only the thought of a soufflé in danger got me here on time!"

Susannah looked swiftly along the table. Madame and Morgan both had a forkful suspended in mid-air. Both lowered their eyes without an exchange of glances. She was certain they did not like Louis's secrecy about his visit to the daaler's. Why? He hadn't tried to hide that so-noticeable Mini. But that wouldn't mean a thing, because he'd expect them to take the directions he'd been given. But they had taken a short cut. Botheration, it was all too stupid.

They took Tante Elise back to the Bay, packed their overnight bags, left mid-afternoon. It was fifty miles, mostly hill, to Christchurch, and Morgan had some stuff to pick up there, mostly veterinary supplies, which he'd get sooner that way, than have it despatched by bus.

"We'll have a snack in town. A one-course meal will do us after a luncheon like that. I'm not having Susannah cooking after a big day like this."

It was as well they had had that snack, for they had engine trouble between Dunsandel and Rakaia, and though a passing car stopped and offered to send a mechanic back from Rakaia, it proved a major fault, entailing a tow to the garage and a two-hour wait there. They were entertained during that time at the manse next door, which was better for Clothilde, but they were all weary when they reached home. Susannah decided her questions regarding Louis could wait another day.

Clothilde was amazingly bright next morning, so Susannah was pretty sure that whatever had been worrying Tante Elise and Morgan hadn't been passed on to her. Morgan would tell her in his own good time. He'd have things to catch up on this morning.

He went down to Dan's place as soon as he finished

breakfast. Louis had just come down. "Any jobs a textile peddler can help with this morning, Morgan?"

"I'll see what Dan's got in mind. I won't be here. That job on the car wasn't finished to the mechanic's satisfaction. It was to get us home, that's all. I'm taking it down. It will be a lengthy job."

Susannah said, "Shall we come down for the run, and bring you back? Then run down tomorrow for it?"

He shook his head. "Thanks, but I've things to see to in Rakaia, anyway. I've got to make arrangements to have the stumps of the old macrocarpa pulled out and the headmaster wants to see me about the Pet Show next month."

Louis said, "If it's just Clothilde you're thinking of, and would rather do those things another day, take Shanna's offer and I'll look after tante."

"Thanks all the same, Louis, but I've put off doing those things for ages. Something else always crops up and I don't get them done. This'll prod me into seeing about them. Those stumps are unsightly. The sooner they're out the better."

Susannah though it would have been more natural for Louis to offer to follow Morgan. He liked driving.

When Morgan got back from seeing Dan he said, "Dan could do with your help in about half an hour, Louis. He's cutting out a mob from Swagman's Gulley and could do it quicker with help."

Susannah expected Morgan to leave immediately, but twenty minutes later he was still there. To her look of surprise he said, "I'd an urgent letter to do first. They can't start the car till eleven. They've got a part coming down on the bus from Christchurch. They had to put a secondhand one in last night."

The phone rang in the office. Morgan picked it up, said, "Yes, Blair speaking, but just a moment before you put him on, will you?" He put his hand over the receiver. "Do you know where Louis is?"

"Yes, I just saw him cross the yard to saddle up. Do you want him?"

"No, this is a private call and I don't want him around."

Susannah picked up her lambswool duster and disappeared. As she went out of the door she heard Morgan say, "Right, Frank, what time shall I meet you?"

Frank? He always called François Rossignol Frank. But of course there were two or three Franks about. In fact, one brother of the tree-felling firm was Frank. Though she'd thought it sounded like a person-to-person call. However, it could have been an office girl at the Rakaia garage, so not a toll-call. It would only be that Louis was so nosey about farm prices. Who'd have thought it? Of course his experiences in life hadn't been the happiest. To be the only member of his family left, then to be deprived of climbing, was enough to embitter anyone and perhaps possessions and money were looked on as compensations.

Shortly Louis came back. "I've seen Dan. He says to tell you we won't be in for lunch. He wants to see Brent about something, so we're going to ride over there first and bring back the mob late this afternoon. *Au revoir.*"

As the sound of hoofbeats died away down the track, Morgan said, "Is Clothilde upstairs? Well, I'll just run up and say goodbye."

Susannah wandered out to the car, all ready to go, in the stableyard. When he came out she said, "I hope it doesn't let you down on the way."

"Very little chance of that. But I'd like the new part in."

Susannah said, "Morgan, there's nothing wrong, is there?"

She thought there was the vaguest hesitation before he answered, as if he almost decided to tell her something. It was over in a flash and he laughed. He opened the car

door, and said, "Not a thing wrong, Susannah. Nor is
there going to be anything wrong from now on between
you and me. I won't permit it. We've got to do some
talking . . . after the reunion, like I said. Till then, the
order of the day is this: a chaste salute upon your maiden
cheek. . . ."

He stooped, kissed the cheek, then got into the car. As
the engine sprang to life Susannah decided to go one
better . . . to his immense surprise. She leaned in, kissed
him on the mouth, said, "That's one for the road." Their
eyes met and they knew a great reluctance to part. Then
he was gone, and neither of them knew that in that
moment of hesitation earlier, he had made the wrong
decision.

As Susannah came in, she heard Clothilde singing. She
went upstairs to make the beds. Oh, how nice, Louis had
made his. She took a pleasure in making Morgan's,
folding the sheet back with precise care, smiling at the
photo of his mother and father on the dressing-
table . . . noting with sheer affection that even last night,
tired and all as he must have been, he had still dipped
into his Palgrave's *Golden Treasury* of poetry. Oh, how
she liked a man who was fond of poetry! The book was
open—what had he been reading? The next moment she
chuckled. It was the section devoted to love-poems, fine
ones, Herrick's, Jonson's, Sedley's.

She replaced it carefully, upside down. There was a
scribbling-pad and ballpoint there, too, written over and
over with many scorings-out. Morgan must still write his
nonsense verses. But she mustn't pry.

Happiness was seeping into her. Oh, how she wished
this wretched reunion was over! As from the day after
tomorrow, they were really going to be plunged into a
whirl of final arrangements. She tapped on her
grandmother's door, was bidden to come in. The bed was
made, so Susannah began to dust. "My, aren't you the

happy one this morning," she teased grand-mère, "singing love-songs so soon after breakfast!"

"And why wouldn't I be doing just that? After what I saw down in the stableyard? I heard the car start and looked out to wave goodbye."

Susannah coloured.

Old Clothilde said, "Don't mind me, child. It makes me very happy. This is as it should have been long ago. But you both had so much pride—formidable pride. You, because you thought Morgan stepped in just to save your face, Morgan because no man wishes to catch a woman on the rebound."

Susannah's eyes widened, then narrowed. She caught Clothilde's arm. "Grand-mère, could that possibly be true? The last bit? Or do you just read into that what you want to read?"

Clothilde looked saucy. "There is only one way of finding out, isn't there? That is to ask him. Have courage, *petite*. There are things I could tell you that would convince you, but I would not rob Morgan of the sweetness of telling you all he should himself."

"We've come so near it, grand-mère. But when the reunion is over . . . ."

Clothilde sighed and seemed to address the whole room, like a player on a stage delivering a soliloquy. "Me? I do not understand this generation at all . . . surely they can realise there is no ideal time for a confession of love? . . . that sometimes the crowded hour, the snatched moment, is sweeter by far. No, I do not understand them!" Then she turned, laughing, to her granddaughter. "Oh, *mignonne*, Morgan has not wanted to rush you this time, he is so afraid of getting the wrong answer. But surely you have enough French blood in you to engineer something that will sweep aside all such doubts?"

Susannah burst out laughing, put her arms about Clothilde and kissed her. "You're a naughty old lady ... but a darling. I'm sure you and Tante Elise talked and plotted the last two days.''

"We did, *chérie*, because while age may dim the sight and dull the hearing, one's inner perceptions are sharpened. We said, the night before last, when you were sitting so close on the window-seat and whispering things we longed to hear, that had we had a magic wand at that moment we would have used it to whisk everyone else away and leave you in a world of two. Now off you go and think on what I have said.''

Susannah was just going in to dust the drawing-room when Stephanie rang for a chat, as she so often did. But after a moment or two she said abruptly. "I've just got to ask you something, Shanna. Morgan seemed a bit worried this morning—didn't seem a bit like himself on the phone. I spoke to him after he spoke to Brent, and Brent was cagey later when I asked him what Morgan said. Do you know anything about it?''

"I thought the same thing. In fact I asked Morgan whether anything was wrong. He said no, but I wasn't satisfied. Stephanie, you said you spoke to Morgan yourself. Did you ask him?''

"I sure did. In the first place I only wanted to ask him something about mother's birthday, but he seemed abrupt, as if he didn't want to discuss that then. I got worried and said, 'What's wrong, big brother? Are things not going too well with you and Shanna?' No, Shanna, don't interrupt. His voice changed immediately and he said, 'In that direction, things couldn't be better, if not finalised between us yet. No, it's something quite different, but it'll work out all right, not to worry. I must go.' But even though he said things were fine, I've worried all the time since. Susannah, I'm probably clumping in where angels wouldn't venture, but oh, please, please, don't break my brother's heart all over again, will you? If he thinks things are working out, make them work out.''

Susannah swallowed. "Break his heart—*again*? What do you mean?"

"I'm going to speak loud and clear. I've a feeling you two got your wires crossed somewhere, somehow, but I don't know the ins and outs of what happened five years ago. I'm sure you aren't indifferent to him. Morgan proposed this earlier reunion to Clothilde just to get you back, if possible. Said perhaps he was a fool, but he'd never been able to get you out of his system, that he'd bungled the whole thing last time.

"It seems when you arrived five years ago he fell in love with you immediately, but you had eyes for no one but John. John was so much nearer your age. Then Morgan told me he'd tricked you into that engagement. Mind you, he couldn't tell me much because he rang me in London, just before we went to Canterbury, and you can't go into details when it's costing a couple of dollars and more a minute. Not that he seemed to care much. But his main purpose was to get you back to New Zealand. He said he'd risk your getting back together with John. I was very doubtful, at first, because what if that was just what happened? I couldn't bear to see anyone else as unhappy as Fran. He said the former engagement had been all a sham, but didn't say why, and said you couldn't get out of it quickly enough later. He said this time there'd be no rush, if only you would come home to stay. He seemed to think you'd be more easily persuaded if I said he was in the New Hebrides—gone from the Vale altogether. Susannah, why did you want to break that engagement, however odd it was? Morgan said that he couldn't hold you to it, he loved you too dearly. What did you say, Shanna?"

"I'm saying, also loudly and clearly, Stephanie, that you're a perfect darling. We did indeed get our wires crossed. I'd been waiting for an opportunity to tell John I was giving him up, that it was just as well we hadn't yet become engaged. I wasn't going to tell him why . . . which was as simple as this . . . I'd realised I'd fallen in love with Morgan. Morgan didn't know that—saw John falling for Fran, and tried to save my face by announcing that we were getting engaged. And then I thought he might just make it reality if I proposed that we break off."

Stephanie burst out laughing. "What a coil! If only I'd known, I'd have shut you up in the Eyrie till you promised to marry each other. But it's working out, isn't it?"

"It is. At Rossignol Bay the other night, in a room full of people, Morgan whispered that when the hoo-ha of the reunion is all over, we'll have things to say to each other."

"Well, if *you* can wait that long, *I* can't. To hell with the reunion; it was only an excuse to get you here, anyway. Shanna, the first chance you get, bring it to the boil again, will you?"

Shanna was choking with laughter. "How unromantic! What would Tante Elise say? But yes, Steph, I'll bring it to the boil!"

She picked up her duster and went back to the drawing-room. She began to dust the huge cabinet along one wall that held the treasures from Old France, and the Colonial ones. These had been brought from England, some of them centuries old. Here in this remote rim of the plains, they'd been part of the life of generations and though some were now very valuable, no special protection had ever been taken for them. There was a key in this lock, but of course a case like this would present no problems to anyone who broke in, in their absence. It was never even turned, but now, on impulse, Susannah turned it and slipped it into her pocket. She told herself it was only because Louis's questions about their probable value had made her conscious of their worth.

She let her eye run along some of the pieces on the shelves . . . if only these things could speak, what tales they would tell! Suddenly her eye was arrested. The sun was shining fully through the curved glass at one end, right on to a long case, black-velvet-lined, on which reposed what grand-mère had said recently was probably the most valuable set of all ... fourteen miniatures, delicately worked. Seven in each of two rows ... but the sun was striking on indentations, blacker than the surrounding velvet ... they had been moved out of place.

Then it hit Susannah. There were no longer fourteen. There were still two symmetrical rows, evenly spaced, but further apart, only six in each! In a flash she knew the truth. Louis had taken them. They would fetch an even greater price overseas than here. No doubt in Papeete, where so many tourists came, they would double in price.

Susannah felt sick. Louis was their kinsman, their beloved Françoise's brother, her own playmate of yesteryear. Her eyes skimmed the shelves feverishly. It wasn't the only thing he'd taken. Oh, but it had been cunning. No big pieces, of course. Nothing noticeable. A patch-box, a snuff-box, one or two tiny ornaments and dishes. She found she was trembling and clenched her hands to stop it.

Thank God he was out with Dan. She wouldn't like to have faced him at the moment. Oh, if only Morgan were home! He would know how to act. They mustn't give grand-mère too much of a shock. Morgan would have to confront Louis, get the things back, get him away so that Clothilde would never know. He must be told to pretend to be called home. At eighty-four her heart might not withstand a shock such as that.

She would ring Morgan, ask him to come home as soon as the car was finished. She'd have to shut herself in the office. Luck was with her. When she went to find Clothilde, she was packing a basket. "I'm going to walk across to Nessie's. I got those chocolate novelties for the children yesterday. I've put some eggs in too. Her fowls aren't laying as well as ours."

Susannah rang the garage at Rakaia. Morgan would be there any moment. He might even come back without having the job done. The man who answered the phone was surprised. "No, Miss Carew, has he had more trouble with the car?"

"No. Perhaps you aren't the one who was dealing with it. The garage is getting a new part down from Christchurch to replace the secondhand part they used last night."

His voice sharpened with surprise. "I did it myself. I didn't use any secondhand part. What is all this?"

She tried again, "But hasn't he got an appointment to bring the car in to you at eleven?"

"He certainly hasn't. There's some mistake."

She felt uneasy, but said, "Well, I've misunderstood him, evidently. But if he should come, would you ask him to ring me. It's rather urgent."

She rang the school, gave the same message, then the tree-fellers. He'd had no appointment there, but then he'd probably just drop in.

She went back up to Louis's room. He'd not been very good at making his bed hitherto. She'd thought it consideration after their late night. But was it possible he didn't want her prying? If Louis *had* taken those things, and she was still so incredulous about it—she still used that "if" in her thoughts—he'd probably have them stowed in his case. Of course they'd been out all day, and the house empty. It could have been burglary.

His case was standing on the floor of his wardrobe and it was locked. How odd to lock a case when staying with relations. She picked it up. It was heavier than she'd expected. It felt as if it was packed with clothes. Two suits, some spare trousers, and a couple of shirts were hanging in the wardrobe, but a week ago that rack had been pretty full of clothes.

She went across to the tallboy. The drawers were empty. There had been no shoes in the bottom of the wardrobe either. No doubt of it, Louis was packed, ready to go.

Now she felt surer of the suspicions she was

entertaining. She went swiftly downstairs. What was the name of that antique shop Louis had visited yesterday morning? Oh, yes. She put the toll call through.

"I wonder if you could tell me if you had a gentleman in about noon yesterday, possibly enquiring about selling you some miniatures and other small pieces, mainly French origin, snuff-boxes, patch-boxes, etc? He would have a very slight foreign accent, tall, and dark."

"Yes and no. He was merely looking around. We got into conversation and he asked the approximate value of such things here. Said he was from France and had such things in his home there. I told him the approximate prices they fetch here and in Christchurch, but told him they would bring more in Paris, London, New York. But tell me, is there something wrong? Are you a police-woman? It sounded so innocuous an enquiry."

She managed a laugh. "Oh, no, there's nothing wrong, just one of the those family arguments. The gentleman in question is a relation of ours and when he told us how much our treasures were worth we hardly believed him."

"Oh," he sounded relieved, "because I never buy anything without careful questioning. I'm not one who buys things more cheaply by asking no questions about their origin."

"I'm sure you aren't. We just thought he was exaggerating."

"I assure you he wouldn't be if he told you the prices I told him. May I advise you, if you have such treasures openly displayed, to have them fully insured?"

She thanked him and hung up, gazing into space. This was something only Morgan could handle. She dared not confront Louis when there was no man in the house. She had no idea what they would do. Probably, for the family's sake, they would demand them back, but not prosecute—he'd trade on that, of course. How despicable!

Her mind flew to the uncomplicated days of fifteen years before, when she had loved Louis as the brother she'd never had. The fun they'd had, the mischief they'd got into, the perils they had survived because he was a daredevil and even then the mountains had a great attraction for him. He'd not realised a girl mightn't have such a head for heights, and it had been Morgan's father who'd rescued her from the cliffs above Forester's Gorge.

Yet the most serious accident had been her fault. She and Louis had been doubling up on the pony when she was teaching him to ride. Tired of the slow jog, she'd urged Twitchy into a gallop. A piece of paper had blown across the track, the pony had shied, and both of them had gone clean over its head on to a barbed-wire fence. Grand-père had rushed them both to Ashburton Hospital to be stitched and have anti-tetanus injections.

Thinking of that made her suddenly revolt against the suspicions she was entertaining. She was letting her imagination run riot. She'd put it out of her mind till Morgan came home. If someone had broken in, he would report it. Possibly he'd ask her to sidetrack Louis till he could get that case open. They mustn't accuse him unjustly. Hard work, that was the thing she needed, something to occupy her.

She'd clean out the storeroom. She armed herself with dusters, floor-cloths, a plastic bucket and soapsuds, a scrubbing-brush. She thought of something, and rang the cottage. "Nessie, could you keep grand-mère there for lunch? I'm tackling some spring-cleaning and I could just make myself a snack and get on."

Nessie was delighted. "My mother's coming this afternoon. She always slips over to the homestead for a chat, so they could have it here instead. Just expect her home about four-thirty."

Susannah worked with a will and made great progress. An hour after her snack she heard hoof-beats. Oh, how hot it was! They were on the verge of summer. Oh, it was Louis. Immediately she felt apprehensive.

He came across the yard whistling. He laughed. "I felt I was more nuisance than I was worth. I was just trying their patience. Brent is going to help Dan. He's worth six of me, so I bowed out gracefully. What are you doing, *chérie*? Scrubbing? Is it necessary in this heat?"

Susannah's suspicions lessened. "I'm almost finished, then I'll shower and change. Grand-mère is at Nessie's for the day. I wouldn't have tackled this if I'd thought it would get so hot. Of course there's not a breath of wind."

"How long will it take you to finish? Not long? Good. Then how about having the first bathe of the year in that pool below the dam? When I saw it the other day I thought it looked most tempting."

It sounded heavenly. "Have you any briefs, Louis? Because if not, I'll hunt you out a pair of Morgan's."

"I haven't. I knew I could borrow a pair of his: I didn't expect to be here as long, and thought the weather wouldn't be right for a warm-blooded Tahitian. I'd forgotten these hot, dry winds of the plains. Don't hurry, I've a business call to put through to Auckland. I'll find out the cost and pay for it."

"Oh, not to worry. I expect the estate can stand it."

"Oh, hardly. Guests can't run up bills like that as well as living on the fat of the land. I asked tante if I could contribute to the household expenses and she wouldn't hear of it, but it's been a lengthy visit."

It gave Shanna a most unreal, almost guilty feeling. How could she entertain suspicions about Louis's honesty when he talked this way?

When she went into Morgan's room, the nor'wester that had sprung up had upset a vase and swirled the scribbling-pad paper all around the rooom. She picked them up, page after page of rough attempts, all scored out and re-written. Then she picked up the last two pages. Not an error on these. Must be the finished product.

Then her own name leapt up at her. That settled it. No girl could resist reading on. She didn't even try to. But she couldn't believe her own eyes. . . .

O poets, had I but the means
When my Susannah dons her jeans,
Of penning how she walks with grace . . .
How in the contours of her face
I find such beauty written there
That none *you* write of can compare!
For Cleopatra of the Nile
Had nothing on Susannah's smile;
Was Mary, Queen of Scots more fair,
With sapphire eyes and auburn hair?
I'll settle for dark honey-gold . . .
O Herrick, though you may behold
Your Julia drest in silken gown,
My love has eyes of greeny-brown,
That lovely curve of throat and chin,
The way one dimple's dented in
Is so distracting; and I find
In her such treasures of the mind.
Jonson might beg his Celia this:
To leave within his cup a kiss,
I'd rather have the sweet surprise
Of laughter in Susannah's eyes;
I'd rather have her scold and chide me
Than all these others here beside me.
I've loved her long, I've loved her well,
O for a poet's art to tell
My wilful love in word and line
That I am hers and she is mine,
That out of all the world I'd choose . . .
Susannah in her denim trews!

Susannah was swept with delicious laughter . . . Morgan and his serio-comic verses . . . but these were sweet. These had the ring of truth. Oh, what a wonderful, wonderful day this was! Oh, Morgan, hurry home! First Stephanie, now this. She picked up the swimming trunks, went to her own room and donned a one-piece chartreuse bathing suit striped diagonally with black. It was too early for a bikini. She slipped a short white towelling jacket over it, and wiggled her toes into sandals.

Louis must have got his call over quickly. He had the estate car waiting. It was a little distance to the pool.

The sun was right on it, the water was deliciously cool, tingling their skins at first because it came down from heights where the air was cooler, in narrow rills that widened out as they met, into this natural basin, hemmed in by a rock barrier, over which the water spilled gently, or seeped through the sides.

It was reasonably safe, provided one kept away from one part where, in heavy rain, branches and even young trees got wedged. But above that, on a ledge of rock, was a perfect place for sunbathing.

They spent half an hour in the water, frolicking, splashing each other, never diving, because it wasn't safe. The bottom was too uneven. Susannah suddenly felt miles above worry level. It was all just too absurd. There was some explanation. Maybe Clothilde could explain the absence of those pieces. Finally, her unease disappeared completely beneath the remembered delight of those absurd verses.

She said, "I'm tired. The first bathe of the season makes you that way. Let's sun ourselves up there. Wish we'd brought the lilos . . . but we can lie on our towels."

It was big enough for four or five persons, that ledge, and the rocks were fairly smooth. They lay face down on their towels, the sun warm on their shoulder-blades. A quarter of an hour later Louis said casually, "By the way, I'll have to take a business trip to Auckland, bother it. I knew it might crop up but hoped I could postpone it till the reunion's over. It could mean a few thousand extra in my pocket for the year if I bring it off. I'll be back for the great day, of course, in fact, long before. I'd not disappoint tante in that for anything. Could you run me in to Christchurch Airport tommorrow morning, really early, Shanna?"

Susannah swallowed, doubts rushing back. She managed, "Of course, Louis. Just how early?"

"Sorry about this ... the eight-thirty. I booked immediately they asked me to come through."

She found her heart was hammering at her ribs. This was it, then. She was probably right about Morgan's business today being connected with Louis. Was it possible Tante Elise had missed something from Rossignol House? ... and Morgan had met François in Chrischurch—halfway—to discuss what they should do?

She didn't think he'd rung Auckland, or the airport. His bag had been packed. He was skipping the country. He'd ring from Auckland to say he had to go straight back to Tahiti. No doubt he'd go on to Los Angeles, sell them there, then, if enquiries were made, he'd profess complete ignorance and indignation. In any case, he would hope they wouldn't be noticed for ages among so many. His luck had been out when that shaft of sunlight had shown the interference this morning. Suddenly she was possessed of a fine anger, but she subdued it. She mustn't let him know she suspected. It gave her a nasty taste in her mouth.

She managed to keep a light conversation going. Finally she raised herself on her elbows and said, "This rock is getting too hard, and anyway, grand-mère may be home now. I think we should make tracks."

"Right. I was just thinking that. Besides, I'd better start my packing. I'm not really anticipating a flight to Papeete to ratify this order, but you never know. I'd better take all."

"Yes, much the best, and it's not as if you brought much." She put a hand up to an overhanging branch to help her to rise. Louis turned over, said, "My word, that must have been quite a gash on your underarm. What caused a scar like that?"

It was between her elbow and armpit and was never apparent unless she raised her arms above her head. She boggled at him. "Louis, you couldn't have forgotten *that*? The pony throwing the two of us on to the barbed wire and grand-père rushing us to hospital?''

Something flickered in the dark eyes and he looked away. He said quickly, "You know how it is, Shanna. Some things I remember, some I forget. This is one of the forgotten things.''

"But surely, when you look at your own scar, so much worse than mine, you'd ask some friend what had caused it?''

She caught at the arm nearest her, turned it over, then her gaze became transfixed, unbelieving. The flesh was tanned, seamed with blue veins . . . and nothing else. Not even the vestige of a scratch, much less a scar.

She shook her head as if to clear it, then with one bounding movement came to her feet. He scrambled to his, made an inarticulate sound—the first time she'd ever seen him at a loss. She was gazing at him with wild incredulity. "It isn't you! I mean, you aren't Louis! But who *are* you? And how come you are here? Why, why are you pretending to be Louis?''

The next moment, at the ugly look on his face, a look which the young Louis could never have worn, she regretted her accusation. He seized her wrists in an iron grip. "You're going to be sorry you did that," he said between his teeth. "If you think I'm going to let you spoil it all now, you can think again. And it is you who are to blame . . . you who called me Louis. I was just going to lie low here. If you hadn't welcomed me like that I'd have been away in a few days.''

She was wide-eyed . . . if she kept him talking, she might get away from him. This was a nightmare, the sort of thing that only happened to other people. And never on a quiet country estate. "But why come to us at all? And why are you the living image of Louis? Who are—'' Then it hit her. She said with conviction, "You're Louis's cousin, no relation to us at all. The one Louis said was always being taken for his twin. Françoise mentioned you years later. She said the likeness was a thorn in Louis's flesh, because you had a record." She twisted violently, caught him off guard because he'd been listening intently to find out how much she might know; she got one wrist free but not the other. With the freed hand doubled into a fist she struck at his chest.

He teetered above that dangerous pool full of snags, with waterweed binding it all together, and instinctively she clutched him to save him. He regained his balance by clinging to her and the next moment she was falling herself. She didn't know whether she'd been pushed or not. Her scream rang out, she struck the water in a whirling of clutching hands and helpless limbs, and with a cold wave of horror, heard him laugh and knew she could expect no help from that quarter.

She held her breath, went under, felt herself slipping between slimy tree-trunks, grabbed, found twigs, held to them desperately, found a toe-hold for a springing-up place, and shot to the surface. She shook her head, dashed the water from her eyes, took in a great gulp of air, turned and saw him there. Never had she seen such a look on any face. It wasn't far to the bank that was safe, where they'd gone in, but he could be there before her and . . . although it seemed incredible, she was instinctively sure she would not be allowed out of the water to reach the homestead and reveal him for what he was.

Panic invaded her, then some strong sense of self-preservation made her turn and make for the opposite bank. Not a friendly bank, this—steep sloping rocks, green with slime, but branches dipped over the water and could help her conquer their slipperiness. She clutched one, looked over her shoulder. He was wondering what to do.

He looked up the hill above that bank and realised that if she got out of the water, she could climb it, possibly make her way through that dense bush to the Gorge Homestead . . . it was in the opposite direction to the Vale, but she could summon help there. He couldn't get around to this bank, but she saw his intent to cut her off, as he struck up above the ledge to reach easier going and drop down to her.

She must get ahead of him. It was her only chance. Desperation lent her strength. She clawed her way up those rocks, fled into the trees. She knew this terrain, he didn't. The trouble was he was above her, and that was the only way there was a path to the Gorge; farther down, the river barred the way. But if she could hide from him, she could make it, later.

Great tree fuchsias leaned down, from the sides of the banks, their gnarled branches giving the right hold ... roots of forest giants provided footholds for her. Sometimes she slipped back, but she knew his progress would be more difficult, steeper, and denser with tangles and thickets of vines and creepers and supplejacks. Her feet would be lacerated to agony point, but the instinct to preserve her life—because she was sure it was in danger— kept her going. She could hear the crashing of his progress, hear him swearing. She saw great red weals appearing on her arms, felt thorns lash at her shoulders, but on she went, her breath coming gaspingly but not daring, yet, to pause for respite.

She gained the shoulder of the hill, found a rain-cleared strip that led down towards the flow of water in the gulley. Desperately she slid down, till she was pulled up by the huge clay-encrusted roots of a fallen beech, a giant of a tree.

She slithered around it and hid behind the great circle of uprooted earth. She lay, filling her tortured lungs, and trying to listen above the thumping of her heart. It quietened a little, and from the sound he was almost at the top of his higher bank. When he gained it, he would try to force his way down to her, if he could hear her.

She looked down at the flow of the water below .... the water she must cross to get to the other side before she could climb the next forested hill that lay between her and the Gorge homestead. Her heart failed her. She'd never make it. Louis, like a true Tahitian, was a magnificent swimmer. She was only medium good. Once he saw her take to the water, he would catch her up, and in this exhausted condition, nothing would save her.

Her eye lit on a large boulder at her feet, and with the sight came inspiration. She acted upon it immediately. It had to be instant because he must be nearly at the top, and she'd have to stand up for this. She picked up the stone, balanced it against her shoulder, then flung it with all her might into the stream below. Before it hit the water she uttered the most bloodcurdling scream of sheer terror she could produce. The sound of it chilled even her own senses. Then she lay flat under the mass of roots and branches. He'd take that for a death-cry as she lost her footing and hurtled down.

She heard him gain the top. He was nearer and lower than she'd thought. He couldn't possibly see her, but she was petrified with fear. Then the crashing started again; he was coming down. It stopped again, and she heard him talking to himself. She heard pebbles failing on to rock, and thought he was going out on to that flat outcrop of rock that overhung the stream, to have a good look to see if she had come to the surface. Just a few yards below that point were some falls, not deep, but forceful and dangerous. He would hope she'd gone over them and been washed out into the river.

Above the sound of the water she heard him give a great sigh of relief. It was quite horrible. She heard him making his way along the bank, evidently making sure she'd not been washed up. She peered out fearfully from the matted roots and saw him scanning the far bank, then, with enormous relief, because by now he was below her, making escape impossible, he retraced his steps the way he had come. The real Louis had know every inch of this ground, even as she did, but this impostor wouldn't.

He went straight up and over where he had emerged. He would be making his way back to the estate car and would make a quick getaway now. He must be in much more serious trouble than what was practically little more than petty theft. The sounds of his progress died away completely. Shanna knew what she must do ... work her way around past the falls, and swim the not-very-formidable distance across the stream, diagonally, to where she knew was a good landing-place, a sandy river-beach. From there it would take her only twenty minutes or so to the swing bridge across the Gorge, and though John was in Wellington, the Raymonds would be there and would contact Dan and Brent. Oh, God send that grand-mère stayed late at Agnes's! Better far they lose the heirlooms than harm come to her.

CHAPTER TEN

It was the unbearable thought of her grandmother meeting that unpredictable usurper that got Susannah out of her hiding-place at last. If he was coming back to have another look, she would hear him. She crawled out and kept very low till she reach the bank below the falls.

Her toes were torn and bleeding, the arches of her feet raw, and she ached in every limb, but she was alive, alive, and she could have been down in that pool, trapped with tangled branches, for Morgan and Dan and Brent to find, hours later.

She had swum across this point several times. The current made it easy; it carried you along to the other side. It was heaven to be in the water, and no longer treading on sharp stones and bush-thorns and tumbling over tree-roots and nettles.

She felt the current taking her a little faster than usual, but that would be her exhaustion and state of mind. She must strike out against it a little if she were to reach the spot she wanted to. Suddenly she realized that she wasn't going to make it, that she was going to be swept out into the Waimauku itself. This wasn't just fatigue; the current was stronger than of old ... wasn't it always said: never say you know a New Zealand river? They changed after every flood. But in any case, it was something she'd still have had to attempt, though she'd have struck out across the current from the start.

She had a moment of extreme panic, then steadied herself ... the river wasn't particularly high, there were all those shingle banks intersecting the branches of even the main stream ... she must make for one. One of the Acland women had done just that, while the men ran up and down the bank fearing her drowned. But of course, they'd seen her swept away. No one, save that impostor, knew anything about this. The next moment she was out into the Waimauku and the next realised with gladness she was being borne towards Dumpling Island. She raised her head, saw the water was swirling in to a little bay with willow and broom above it, and stuck out with renewed strength, not daring to lose momentum by putting her feet down to try to touch bottom, even when she was very near, and not till her knees painfully scraped river shingle did she know she was safe.

She crawled up the bank, found soft river silt, and lay there panting. Then, fearful lest in any way Louis's cousin could be on the watch, crawled under a willow that leaned over the bank. She was so exhausted and chilled the sand felt incredibly warm against her body. When she felt revived, she scanned the opposite shore, saw no dread figure, and flitted like a pale ghost through the scrub to what would save her from exposure ... the old hut built there after that long-ago party had been marooned.

She stumbled in, caring not that it was musty, that cobwebs hung in eerie veils, and that it was dark because it had only two tiny windows. It was shelter, and safety, and tonight she would be rescued because she would be able to light the lamp, and they would investigate. In fact, even before then, she hoped, because once Morgan was home, and pray God she would be able to see from here

his car cross the bridge, she just might be able to to
attract attention. She dared not risk it before Morgan
reached the homestead. Better by far that the impostor
get away, without disturbing her grandmother, than that
he find out she had not perished in the waters.

Meanwhile there were basic provisions here. Tinned
milk, an opener, biscuits, baked beans, tea, coffee. She
dared not light a fire yet, though. She spooned some of
the sweet condensed milk into her, unsealed the biscuits.
Manna, they were, even if stale. But best of all were the
blankets, tightly lidded in a chest against flies, incredibly
musty, but dry and warm.

Huddled in them she pulled up a chair to watch for
signs of Morgan's return. To her great joy she found she
could see the bridge, and the stable-yard, and part of the
homestead. Oh, the matchless comfort of these
rugs . . . Susannah went out like a light.

She woke to pitch darkness and a great sense of guilt.
She had not kept her vigil. She was warm now, blessedly,
restoringly warm. Fear shook her. What might have
happened at the homestead in her time of unconscious-
ness? Had that man gone? What would they have
thought when neither of them showed up? Would they
have searched and found her bathing suit missing?
Would they have missed the estate car?

She dragged herself out of her cocoon of blankets,
stumbled to the window, looked across the river. Not
only was the homestead a blaze of lights, but all over the
hillsides were moving dots of light, torches and lanterns
carried by searchers, people with dread in their hearts,
looking for Clothilde's darling granddaughter, mourn-
ing her as probably drowned, hoping against hope she
had been washed ashore and had survived, as indeed she
had.

She felt her way to the table with the kerosene lamp on
it and the matches in the tin. She removed the glass by
the match-light, and lit the wick, replacing the glass. She
mustn't turn it up quickly, but let the glass get used to

heat first. She wished it was an old storm-lantern rather than a table-lamp. That would be better for signalling with.

She lit the dry pine-needles and cones piled up in the rough fireplace. Their resinous quality flared up immediately, and she piled on driftwood from an old carton. The room was immediately filled with light . . . oh, if only that window on the homestead side were larger . . . but they must notice it, surely. When the fire was in no danger of going out, she would go outside, move the lantern to and fro. Oh, if only she had some clothes—this bathing-suit felt frightful, the straps were cutting into her shoulders, the legs chafed her at every step. Her teeth chattered.

She moved to the cutlery drawer in the old table—ah, an old knife, dagger-sharp, would do it. She inserted the point into the middle of the thin grey blanket, ripped, then tore it.

She wrapped it around her sarong-fashion, above her bosom, and tucked the top corner in tightly. Oh, how much better! She made her way in the light of a pale, weary-looking moon to the bank nearest the homestead. She waved her lamp gently to and fro. Still the moving circles of light weaved from one side to the other on the hillsides and gullies above Larchwood. By listening intently she could hear their calls; they were crying out: "Shanna! Shanna!" over again. Not "Louis." Then he must have got away. Perhaps he had left a note, hoping to the last he would not be known for what he was. He might even have said she was going for a bathe, and he'd had an urgent call to Auckland.

A chill wind that came right off the mountain-tops was sweeping right down the riverbed, making it useless for her to shout in the pauses when the searchers stopped calling her name. They were waiting for an answer from the banks of the pools they used for swimming, not the river. The river-silt was working into the cuts and scratches on her feet. Oh, how long, how long before she attracted their attention? She tried for a higher piece of land, and stood squarely on a piece of gorse, causing her to cry out with pain. Then she thought: gorse! Nothing more inflammable!

She stumbled back for matches and kerosene. What a blaze she would make! She found her way back to the gorse-bush, held her lamp high to make sure it was a big one, and dry . . . it was. She stood on the windward side of it, let the kerosene trickle sparingly over the branches, put her match to it, then had to spring back as it roared to life—oh, what a wonderful sight!

She strained her ears and eyes into the darkness . . . suddenly she heard a shout, then answering shouts, and knew her beacon had been seen. They started to shout, but where she had been able to distinguish her own name, this was just a blur. But never mind, they would investigate. Then, blessedly, came the sound of a loud-hailer. They must have a police-car or a traffic-car there. "You on the island . . . " it said, "are you Shanna Carew? Are you Shanna Carew? If you are, wave your lantern twice horizontally, and twice vertically."

It was repeated immediately, but before they'd got halfway through she was doing as she was bid. The voice cut off and a great cheer went up, repeated in diminishing effect from all over the hillsides. Another message: "Are you quite all right? Answer as before." She repeated the waving. A silence, possibly for consultation. Then, "We have to get a boat from Blair Hills. A boat from Blair Hills. Do you understand this?" Then lastly, "Go into the hut and keep warm. It may take half an hour. Answer if you understand it may take half an hour." She signalled. The voice said, "Message ends. Just keep warm till . . . ." Then another voice reached her. "Message doesn't end, Susannah. I'll be with you soon." Morgan's voice. He was there. He was home. Now all she needed to know was . . . his voice came over again. "Your grandmother sends her love. See you soon."

The Blairs were the only ones who kept a boat these days. They used it on a small lake on the property for trout-fishing. They'd have to get it on the trailer before conveying it to the river. It would be more like an hour. But did that matter?

She went up to the hut, set the lamp down. The fire she had piled up with big logs was sending out a terrific heat now. She felt renewed now that help was at hand, that her grandmother was safe. She took the old black kettle, found the light from the moon stronger now, enough to light her way down to the river.

She rinsed it out several times, filled it, brought it back to set on the swing hob over the flames. She made a huge pot of tea, sat with her hands wrapped around the hot mug, drank two scalding mugfuls, munching biscuits in between. It helped pass the time. No good straining one's eyes out the window. The boat wouldn't have a light, anyway. She dragged the indescribable but comfortable old chair to the fire, and sat there, sticking her feet out to the blaze.

Then she heard the most extraordinary noise for an uninhabited island in the middle of a vast Canterbury river . . . she heard a horse whinny! Then the jingle of bridle and bit . . . and the next moment Morgan's big bulk filled the open space as he wrenched the door open and his voice said, "Susannah . . . oh, Susannah, sweetheart . . . ." and he gathered her to him blanket and all. Before he kissed her he said, "Are you all right, *mignonne*? My heart's darling, are you all right? Are you, are you?"

She sagged against him. "I am now. Now, you've come. Oh, Morgan, Morgan, what did you call me? Is it just because you thought I was drowned? Or do you mean it?" She knew, of course, from reading those verses, but he must, he must tell her.

"Mean it? Mean it? Susannah, I've loved you quite desperately for five years in spite of trying to stop loving you all the time you stayed away. As soon as you came

here for that last reunion, I loved you. I couldn't get over
the fact that the dear little girl of twelve I was so fond of
had grown into a woman of twenty-two who made my
blood leap. I thought you'd think me too old, and at first
you had eyes for no one but John. Susannah, can't you
remember that day up in the box-room when we read
Victorine Rose's letters? How I stopped myself then, I
don't know. It seemed so caddish when everyone was
sure that by the time we had the reunion, you'd be
engaged to John.

"He was so much nearer you in age, but many was the
time I thought: To hell with behaving like a gentleman . . . I ought to have swept you off your feet there and
then, because what happened? He turned from you to
Fran, poor Fran . . . and you seemed to just look on me
as a stop-gap, a chivalrous sort of bloke who'd saved
your face. It was nothing of the kind; it was sheer
opportunism. I hoped against hope that in time you
might look my way, but no . . . the moment the reunion
was out of the way and John and Fran's engagement
announced, you couldn't get rid of me quickly enough. I
didn't want a reluctant wife . . . I'm a primitive sort of
chap at heart, Susannah. I wouldn't share even your
thoughts with any other man." He had punctuated every
sentence with a kiss. Now he said, "Darling, what are
you trying to do? Break away from me?"

She laughed, a laugh of sheer happiness. "No, no, no!
I just want enough breath to tell you something in return.
I'd never have spent all those years away, eating my
heart out for you, if I'd had the faintest glimmering you
felt like this. Oh, Morgan Hervington-Blair, if only you
hadn't seen me watching John and Fran in the
shrubbery that day . . . if you'd waited just twenty-four
hours later, you'd have known I didn't love him. I'd
made up my mind to tell him that night I wanted to call a
halt to our relationship, our tepid, petering-out relationship . . . know why? Because I'd fallen in love with you,
madly, irresistibly, once-for-ever, in the box-room. I

thought you still carried a torch for Marty, and that was why you'd never married, that you'd never look on me as anything move than a freckled little tow-haired brat of twelve. I mean . . . Morgan, you'd once spanked me. How could I dare hope your gesture had been anything more than a kind one?"

He laughed. "Actually Stephanie, running at my side, gasped out most of this to me in the last few ghastly hours, but I wanted to hear it from you." Again he laughed, the sort of laugh she'd never heard from him before—tender, exultant, believing—and she said, "Oh, Morgan, kiss me again so I know it's true."

"If only you'd stop talking long enough to get your mouth in the right shape, I'd oblige." Then, all laughter gone, "Oh, Susannah, Susannah, I thought you had drowned." He shuddered violently, then his lips came down on hers.

When at last he lifted his head, he picked her up, and sat down with her in the old chair. "Nothing like these old plush Victorian chairs with spreading laps to accomodate two people. Oh, if only Tante Elise could see us! She wanted an idyll for us . . . with lavender growing and soft sea-winds blowing. And what have we got? A filthy hut and my bride-to-be looking like Ophelia, all witchlocks and river-weed. My darling, are you really all right? Let me look at you."

He undid the blanket still tied around her, saw in the light of the fire her scratched and bleeding shoulders, great lumps on her legs from the nettles, the scraped and filthy feet, and said brokenly, "Oh, Susannah, forgive me. It's all my fault. I ought to have warned you. I . . . ."

She reached up, put her hands about his face, said, "Oh, Morgan, how could it be your fault? Oh, I was so foolish. You see, Morgan, Louis isn't Louis. He's his wicked cousin on his mother's side. And he—" She shuddered.

"Darling, I know. He's Armand de Courcy. Let me tell you. I felt for some time there was something odd, so at variance with Louis's character at fifteen, or fourteen or whatever it was. I never knew about that cousin, but Tante Elise did. I felt it was odd he forgot some things that ought to have been second nature, like riding for instance. But with Elise it was a sudden revelation.

"Remember they were talking about there being no resemblance between Louis and his sister? Tante began to say something and stopped, changing the subject. She'd started to stay she'd seen a resemblance to Fran in the turn of Louis's head, the shape of his hands, and his pointed Rossignol ears. As she got nearly to the last, she looked directly at Louis's ears—I mean Armand's. Ears don't change, she said to me. Shanna and Louis and François and I all had those ears.

"Her self-possession was remakable in an old lady. But she had already puzzled over something. Louis is a shocking letter-writer, we know, but it seems once in a while he did write to Elise, who is a Rossignol by birth as well as marriage, of course, whereas Clothilde is neither. When she heard of his accident she wrote him and in his reply he said he was lucky he had no head injuries at all, just his leg. Said he'd be climbing again before too long. He's in the Andes right now—not that we knew that then. But Armand did, so knew he was safe for a while. Tante Elise laid a trap yesterday morning—showed him a piece that Margot's employer in London sent her as a wedding-present. Not a Rossignol heirloom, but a vauable piece, seeing she's an antique dealer.

"Elise said, 'I'm sure you'll recall this, Louis, because you had the twin of it at home before misfortune caused your father to sell it. One was given to your branch of the family, one to ours. Françoise was so taken with this, I promised her I'd leave it to her in my will.' Armand fell right into the trap, said he remembered the other one perfectly, and how Françoise had written home about it. Then she was sure he was Louis's renegade cousin.

"Frank Rossignol rang the Papeete police last night, to make enquiries. This time he was pushing drugs under cover of a spoof textile business. A young man met his death through them. Armand was in Los Angeles when he heard, and didn't dare return. He switched planes in the most cunning way, came to Auckland, and on the way remembered his cousin talking of this place as the back of beyond. He thought he'd hole up here for a while because Louis was out of touch. Armand was only going to trade on the relationship, hoping Louis had never mentioned his misdeeds.

"But you, naturally, mistook him for Louis and we all followed suit. It was fifteen years since anyone here had seen him, and who would have thought of such a masquerade? He seized the opportunity—these chaps who live by their wits are very quick on the uptake. The accident provided him with a great excuse for not remembering some things. He was very clever. Louis must have told him, at some time, about some of your escapades—just enough to make him sound authentic.

"Frank said the Christchurch police wanted to see me this morning. Frank was there too. Enquiries were being set in motion, but naturally the machinery between two countries, as regarding the law, has to grind slowly and correctly. I was to return home, behave as normal, and the police would be in touch as soon as certain things were in order. My great mistake was in saying nothing to you this morning, also in not saying enough to Brent and Dan. I just said to Brent I'd be grateful if he kept Louis busy, and the same to Dan, because he was a bit meddlesome and such a greenhorn in stock matters he was a bit of a menace. Not enough to make them keep him by them all the time. They could hardly have held him with them anyway, without arousing his suspicions. Besides, I didn't know it was really serious till I got to Christchurch. Frank was guarded in case Armand picked up the extension. And I was afraid to make you act unnaturally with him.

"I arrived back to find him getting into the estate-car with his suitcase and knew he'd rumbled us. Thank God

Clothilde was still at Nessie's and Brent and Dan had just arrived with the mob. I asked Armand where he was going. He spun a tale about being called to Auckland, said you'd told him to drive up, and next day you'd get Agnes to drive up with you in the Hunter, that both of you would do some shopping and one of you would drive the parked one back. Then he added, when I asked where you were, that you'd gone bathing, that you'd spring-cleaned the storeroom and wanted to cool off. I accepted that, but thought Elise must have given her suspicions away and he was off.

"Then suddenly I saw his hands were covered with scratches. That was my worst moment . . . to date. I thought a hideous thought . . . savvy?" She nodded. "I thought he had other vices we didn't know about, that in defending yourself you'd used your nails.

"Brent and Dan thought I'd gone mad, but at least I got a measure of the truth out of him. I sprang on him, told him I knew he was Armand, not Louis, and that I knew what he was wanted for. I almost choked him . . . just gave him enough breath to tell me what had happened."

Susannah said, incredulously, "You don't mean he told you that he pushed me into the pool—wouldn't let me get out on that side?"

Morgan's eyes were intent on hers in the leaping firelight. "He said you'd gone bathing together, but that you'd disappeared among the snags, and he knew he'd get blamed for not saving you, and that it would come out that he wasn't Louis and he was off." Morgan looked guilty for a moment. "It was then that Brent and Dan had to haul me off him. They actually tied him up. Then Brent rang the Christchurch police while Dan and I went racing up to the pool. Your towel was still there." His face went bleak, remembering. "We stripped off and dived and dived and searched and searched. Then we went right down the waters of that gulley, praying that if in some miraculous way you had come to the top and over, you might have reached the bank. The Christ-church police sent out the Ashburton boys ahead of them. They organised the search and rescue teams. Oh, *mignonne*, how did you get here?''

Susannah told him the whole story, and again he shuddered. When he recovered he said, ''Your grand-mother has been magnificent. Her face was carved in sorrow, but she kept fires going, muttering, 'She *must* be found, she *must* be found. . . .' and she herself made endless cups of tea for the searchers, with Edie and Nessie, and my mother, of course. But you're here, and it's a miracle . . . Susannah, after that time we spent with Elise in her garden, before she told me about this, I knew we couldn't wait for the hoo-ha of the reunion to be over . . . then this had to happen. At intervals, in my mad searching I kept thinking that at least you knew I loved you—when Stephanie told me—but what use would that be now? And you would never know how I loved you! Or how much!''

Susannah giggled. ''But I do. More than Cleopatra was loved . . . more than Herrick's Julia . . . Morgan, tell me one thing, did Mary, Queen of Scots have blue eyes? I know she had red hair. Everyone knows that. But the eyes?''

Morgan looked at her as if she'd taken leave of her senses.

''What—oh, my burblings on my scribbling pad? You read it? No, of course I didn't know what colour the Queen's eyes were, poet's licence, my love. It fitted the metre. It's just a jingle, you know. You must never show it to anyone who can really write poety.''

Her eyes were soft. ''Morgan . . . in your extravagance you made me outshine all those women the poets have written of through the ages, you absurd man! I'm going to be the same about you . . . that poem, for me, outshines any Poet Laureate's, outshines Shakespeare's Sonnets, any word that has ever been written.''

In their mutual laughter was the promise of happy

years to come, spent at the Vale, with their family about them, Clothilde's great-grandchildren. . . .

Morgan said, taking her to the window, "By the concentration of lights on the far bank, I think they're launching the boat. Grey Lady will ford the river after us. Darling, we've very little time left together for the rest of this night. It will belong to other people. But there's one thing I want to get straight before we're rescued."

Susannah looked panicky. "Morgan, no. Surely there can't be anything more to be explained away between us. Please don't say—"

"It's not controversial, my love. I'm simply laying down an ultimatum. It's this: I'm done with waiting. The reunion isn't going to hold us up."

"Of course not. We'll tell them tonight. I've got my lovely emerald ring—it's in my bedroom. I'll put it on and we can tell everyone we're engaged again."

The sherry-brown eyes crinkled into laughter. "I'm not referring to an engagement. I'm referring to our wedding. We've wasted enough of our lives. Christmas follows on the heels of the reunion . . . if you think I'm waiting till the New Year, you're absolutely mistaken."

She gazed at him in amazement. "But Morgan, weddings take organising. Oh, darling, I'd like to rush over to the Manse right now and be married, but you know, grand-mère and mother and father will want a big day, and your parents, and Stephanie and—there's a wedding dress to be made and—"

"Wedding dress nothing! Like Tante Elise said, it's there in a glass case at Rossignol House . . . ready and waiting, Victorine Rose's wedding gown, waiting to be worn by Susannah Rose."

"You chump . . . they had back-lacing stays in those days, and wasp waists. It would be impossible."

"It won't be. You must remember Clothilde wore it when she married your grandfather. They must have let it out. We aren't waiting for any dressmaking. Your parents will be here for the reunion, so that's it, my love.

What could be more opportune? . . . and you'll remember I'm an opportunist by nature. Just think of it, all catering arranged for already . . . a shipmates' wedding. Oh, look, they're putting out the boat. See, they're steering by a very powerful torch.''

She clutched him. ''Morgan . . . is Armand there?''

''No, love. I forgot to tell you. The other charges can't be laid yet of course, but they're holding him on the theft charges.''

She was content then. Morgan's father was first out on to the beach. Susannah was swept up into a mighty embrace. She felt his tears against her own cheek. Then Morgan said, ''Dad, I'll have you know you're squeezing the life out of your daughter-in-law-to-be!''

Stephen Blair said, ''Well, thank God for that. You've certainly taken your time, son,'' and he kissed Susannah again.

The day of the reunion dawned as still as a dream. The guests had assembled the night before . . . nearly every home at Linden Peaks had its quota of spare beds filled, and the shearing-quarters of Blair Hills and Larchwood Vale had every bunk occupied. The garden shimmered with sun and dew. John Forester was away on a trade mission to Australia. The Gorge homestead was up for sale, and the descendant of another shipmate was interested in the property. The last shadow was gone.

Shanna's mother was there to help Clothilde dress the bride. Reporters were there, even TV cameras. The old phaeton that had been a show-piece in one of the stables for years was gleaming from much polishing. It was to take the bride to the chapel on the estate, which, as the central one, had been the place for it to be erected all those years ago, across the roadless plains, just half a mile across the fields. Charlotte and Léonie Rossignol were attending their cousin as bridesmaids, Brent and Dan supporting Morgan.

The Reverend Fergus MacNeill of Linden Peaks

parish was marrying them, just as he had wedded Marty
Reddington and Philip Griffiths nearly fifteen years ago.

Clothilde Larchwood and Elise Rossignol had no tears
in their eyes. Their cup of happiness was full. These two
they loved were bringing a new life and a new generation
to Larchwood Vale.

The organist—Stephanie—received the signal, and
struck up *Praise my soul, the King of Heaven*, and the
congregation rose to its feet and began to sing the first
verse for the entry of the bride.

Morgan, standing with Brent and Dan, turned his
head and saw Susannah behind the Reverend Fergus, on
the arm of her father, coming towards him in deep cream
watered silk, high-waisted and with long hanging sleeves
of guipure lace, and a tiny edging of lace at her slim
throat. She wore not a veil, but, as Victorine Rose had
done more that an century before, a wide-brimmed
Leghorn straw hat, wreathed under the edge with
orange-blossom. A trail of it lay against the dark honey-
coloured hair, and over her gown lay an emerald
pendant, to match the green of her eyes.

Just as Victorine had, she carried a Victorian posy of
cream rosebuds and forget-me-nots. She lifted her eyes to
Morgan's and stepped into place beside him. His eyes
met hers. He smiled. She smiled back, not nervous, but
serene.

Into that hushed moment before the minister began,
"Dearly beloved, we are gathered together ... " fell
little Elise's voice from where she stood between
Clothilde and the older Elise. "Tante, is *this* the
reunion?"

The eyes of the two old ladies met. "It is, my child, in
every way, a reunion," whispered Elise Rossignol.

Don't miss any of these exciting titles.

Complete and mail this coupon today!

Harlequin Reader Service

IN U.S.A.:
MPO Box 707, Niagara Falls, N.Y. 14302

IN CANADA:
649 Ontario St., Stratford, Ontario N5A 6W2

Please send me my FREE Harlequin
Reader Service Catalogue.

Name _____

Address _____

City _____

State/Prov. _____ Zip/Postal _____

003565322

Don't let this chance pass you by!